"What a gorgeous weave this novel is—somehow, with the lightest and most precise of touches, Bakopoulos reveals how lives, families, and countries fall together and apart in this thing we call life. In this one summer in Athens, love and death and art and politics all shimmer and quake, lifting and breaking the heart in equal measure."

—**STACEY D'ERASMO**, author of *Wonderland*

"Bakopoulos writes of expatriates and exiles, immigrants and refugees, with such intimacy, tenderness, and wisdom, intuiting as she does that these are all states of grief. The stoicism with which her characters bear their various losses—portrayed in limpid, pensive prose reminiscent of Rachel Cusk's work—is deeply affecting."

—**PETER HO DAVIES**, author of *The Fortunes*

"*Scorpionfish* is transporting, a finely tuned story about art and friendship and the weight of history. Against the backdrop of the Greek economic crisis, Natalie Bakopoulos depicts Athens and island life with grace and accuracy, telling a story of return at once deeply personal and universal. A moving novel with an unexpected undertow."

—**CARA HOFFMAN**, author of *Running*

"*Scorpionfish* dazzles, fierce and tender in turn. The clarity of its insights about love and loss and grief will break you and remake you. Savor it, and it will leave you changed."

—**JESMYN WARD**, author of *Sing, Unburied, Sing*

"*Scorpionfish* is a riveting, elegant novel keenly observed in the manner of Elena Ferrante and Rachel Cusk. A divine, chiseled stunner."

—**CLAIRE VAYE WATKINS**, author of *Gold Fame Citrus*

SCORPIONFISH

Natalie Bakopoulos

 TIN HOUSE BOOKS / Portland, Oregon

Published by Tin House Books, Portland, Oregon

Distributed by W. W. Norton & Company

Library of Congress Cataloging-in-Publication Data TK

Printed in the USA
Interior design by Diane Chonette

www.tinhouse.com

For Jeremy

Our entire body, like it or not, enacts a stunning resurrection of the dead just as we advance toward our own death. We are, as you say, interconnected. . . . In the most absolute tranquility or in the midst of tumultuous events, in safety or danger, in innocence or corruption, we are a crowd of others.

—ELENA FERRANTE, *Frantumaglia*

PART ONE

1

Mira

The small two-bedroom flat where I lived until I was five is on the northern slope of Mount Lykavittos, between the neighborhoods of Ambelokipi and Neapoli. Back in Athens for the first time since my parents' funeral a few months earlier, my arrival felt both unreal and more real than anything I might have imagined, as though my porous, jet-lagged self had emptied itself into this space.

Aris was working in Brussels for the week, and though I still could have gone straight to his place, I didn't. Though I'd planned to live with him, I had to spend some time cleaning out my parents' flat before I'd rent it out. When I'd come for the funeral I couldn't bring myself to go near it. I expected Aris to object to all this, but instead he'd only asked, "You sure you want to be alone there?" I told him I'd be fine, but really, I wasn't sure.

In fact, it had been so long since I'd been to this apartment that when the cab driver hoisted my bags out of the trunk, he must have noticed my disorientation because he asked, "Is this the right place?" I told him yes, but hesitantly. Then I recognized the flat on the ground floor, which, as when I was a child, had its shutters open to the street. You could have jumped right in from the sidewalk.

I held my jumble of keys like a lantern. It was growing dark, and for whatever reason—crisis, negligence—all the streetlights were out. The key to the apartment itself, a big, old-style safety key, was obvious, but I couldn't seem to locate the one for the building door. The others were for Aris's place, the house on the island, and who knows where else.

A light went on inside, and a tall man, perhaps in his early fifties, wearing headphones and running clothes, came down the staircase. He opened the door for me. I thanked him, acting as if my hands were simply full. Noticing, he helped me haul my suitcases up the first few stairs from the foyer to the elevator on the first floor. Even now, I remember the soapy smell of the rhododendrons by the mailboxes, the hint of his grapefruit cologne.

I followed him, then stopped at the foot of the marble stairs. He, whom I'd later know as the Captain, placed my bags in the elevator and asked me which floor. I told him the third, and a look of surprise crossed his face. "Oh," he said. "We're neighbors."

How had he seen me upon this initial meeting? How had I seen him? I struggle to remember how many of these details I had truly noticed or have simply inserted now. We must have spoken in Greek, though later we'd use English as well. Did I hear the thin music from his headphones? I recall something I had until now forgotten: in that first interaction, I felt a flash of recognition, of some silent acknowledgment, a feeling of both surprise and inevitability.

I thanked him, and when he left I sent the suitcases up—the elevator too small for both me and the bags—and took the stairs. Everything looked smaller than I remembered, but walking up those strange yet familiar flights engaged some sort of homing instinct. As if my arms were moved by some force outside myself, I turned the clunky safety key in the lock and pushed open the door.

Forgetting that my mother had begun remodeling before she died, and that it had looked different even before then, I had expected the apartment of my youth. There was still the airy living room, those high ceilings, the honey-colored parquet floors. A new coat of paint—a soft beige accented with white crown molding. Sheer curtains over the glass doors to the balconies, new shutters. Once closed in and rather dark, the kitchen had been redone in a more contemporary style, as a pass-through with stools and a serving bar, opening up to the dining room. The cabinets were new, white and shiny, and there were new butcher-block countertops. The refrigerator was also new, but affixed to it were a few magnets from take-out souvlaki places, touristy ones from all over the country that my mother, rather inexplicably, had collected.

I remembered more paintings and photographs on the walls, but now only two things remained: a framed print of the entire *Divine Comedy*—all 100 cantos printed in tiny, barely legible font—and a large painting of Nefeli's. The piece, one from a series of variations on an old church near the sea, had once hung in our dining room in Chicago and now hung here, over the dining room table. The last time my parents came to Greece, they'd brought it back with them. The large door of the church was open, and in the doorway stood a woman with a dark mane of hair, her back to the viewer. Almost unnoticeable, blending into the darkness. From afar it looked like a dark painting of a church and nothing more. Sometimes I imagined the girl moving; at one point I had convinced myself that she appeared only to me.

Despite my annual visits, I hadn't been back to the apartment since my father's older sister, Haroula, was alive and living there; over the past seven years I'd always stayed with Aris. After Haroula passed, my parents rented the place; they primarily came during the summers and preferred to stay on N., the island where my mother was born. But last summer, perhaps in anticipation of spending her golden years moving between N. and Athens, my mother began to renovate, as if making these improvements would convince my father to return them to Greece. To her, assimilation was equivalent to death.

I called Aris in Brussels to let him know I'd gotten in safely. He apologized again for not being there. He asked about the apartment, and I told him about the new kitchen, the fresh paint on the walls, the simple furniture. He seemed relieved.

As we were hanging up, he blurted *Hang in there*, which I might have taken as strange, had I not still been mourning my parents. His familiar voice soothed me, though it felt thick with a sadness I attributed, at the time, to the wrong thing.

Few reminders of my parents remained. There was the record player, a smaller version of the one in Chicago, and several end tables. But below the bathroom sink I found a collection of mostly empty liquor bottles—my mother's cashed-out arsenal. I picked one up, unscrewed the metal cap, smelled the thin trace of vodka. I turned around quickly, feeling as though she were watching me. My mother, always the subtext.

I moved through my old apartment as though I could walk through walls, my past and present and future selves all negotiating the same space, bumping shoulders, tripping over feet.

The closets were nearly empty, except for a few storage bins. I was surprised to find papers and notes from when I had been a graduate student in ethnography, taking oral histories, talking to the inhabitants of the island who lived through the Nazi occupation, through the dictatorship. It's how I met first Aris's father—the novelist—then Aris himself. That first meeting with Aris, and then what came after—that is the love story most would want to hear.

*

My next exchange with the Captain happened the following day.

Jet lag had kept me in bed most of the morning, and I felt oddly cold. I could not figure out how to turn on the heat. The thermostat seemed purely decorative. A large monstrosity sat in the corner of the living room, some sort of space heater, but I didn't know how to use it. The relentless chill of a winter in Athens was nothing like Chicago, of course. I'd expect it in January. But this was early May.

When I finally made it out of bed, I slid open the door of the balcony and stepped out into the late-morning sun. The apartment was on the third floor, but because the building was built into the side of the hill, the courtyard plunged down five or six stories. From here I could peer down into the tree tops—a pretty space filled with lemon trees, bitter oleander, and *mousmoulia*, the loquat-like fruits that most reminded me of my grandparents' home in Halandri. The space was spotlessly maintained by the elderly couple who occupied the bottom two floors of the building. The man was sweeping the courtyard, and I could hear his wife talking from somewhere inside. I recognized the cadence of her voice and realized that they had been living there for nearly forty years, if not more. Since I'd been a child. From another apartment I heard a quiet, measured conversation, and from another building the shouts of children playing and the steady pound of a hammer. But street traffic was nearly imperceptible, and it was surprisingly quiet—the rustle of leaves, the chirping of birds.

The Captain and I shared adjoining back balconies that overlooked the courtyard, separated by a wall of opaque thick glass, an architectural veil behind which I heard him now moving from one side of the balcony to the other. I could not see him but felt his presence. He sighed deeply, and for a moment I thought he was going to speak. But it was my voice that first bridged the gap.

"I'm sorry to bother you," I said, in my most polite Greek. "But can you tell me how to turn on the heat?"

"There is no heat." The building had voted to not pay for heat this winter, he explained. The costs were too high. "But this cold is very rare for this time of year," he added reassuringly, noting it would warm up again in the next few days.

He could tell by my silence I did not find this comforting. "I have a few space heaters," he added. "If you'd like them."

"There's one in my living room," I said. "But I'm afraid of it."

He laughed, then apologized, offering to come have a look.

Moments later, the Captain hesitated at the threshold, glancing around, focusing on my table: coffee gone cold, a half-finished beer, a bar of chocolate, my books and pens and papers and laptop. My two suitcases, one of them thrown open in the middle of the dining room. He was taller than I remembered. I realized I looked a little ridiculous, my hair covered in a navy beanie, wearing my father's too-large fisherman's sweater that I had found in a drawer. His eyes were drawn to Nefeli's early painting above the table. "She lived here, years ago," he said. "A friend of my father's. A well-known artist."

I did not reveal my connection to Nefeli then. I can't say why. Though much of it I would later discover he already knew. How my father and Haroula, Nefeli's lover, were siblings. How Haroula had hid her sexuality from my grandparents, despite the years that she and Nefeli had lived here, in this apartment together, a fact I suspect they'd nonetheless known and simply refused to accept. Though I admit a hazy understanding of Greek inheritance laws, I do recall that children should inherit property equally. Some divide it up among themselves, assume ownership for this or that. Haroula died with nothing to her name. She wanted no property. She was against it. "Penniless like Sotiria Bellou," Aris's father, the novelist, used to say. There's a photo in his house on the island of the three of them: he and Haroula and Nefeli dancing around a table, Haroula with her head thrown back in laughter, a black curtain of hair concealing Nefeli's face.

I offered the Captain a drink, some coffee, but he declined. I showed him the contraption in the living room.

"Kerosene," he said. He explained how to light it and I stood back while he did so, as if it might charge us like a wild animal.

11

Then he moved across the room and opened the sliding glass door that led to the balcony. "You have to leave this cracked," he said. "Not safe otherwise."

"Carbon monoxide," he added, in English.

I peered into the heater, at the flame, as if to see how close I could get without getting burned. I rubbed my arms, hugged myself. "Maybe I'll just wear layers and wait for summer." I spoke in English now. His use of it had been an invitation.

"It's really fine. Just leave the window cracked, for venting. The whole place will warm in no time. But again, this cold snap will pass."

As he was headed toward the door, I asked how long he'd lived here. He hesitated. I had not expected it to be a difficult question. "The apartment has been in my family but I've only recently moved back."

"Me too," I said. I did not ask from where, and neither did he. I thought about asking again if he'd like a drink, in the Greek manner of asking—insisting—a million times, but I did not.

*

I could not come and go discretely in this building, and the afternoon was backgrounded by the echo of voices and footsteps on the stairway, the hum of the old elevator, the loud clatter of keys. The jet lag felt really terrible this time, and I could barely move my body, stuck in some sort of torpor. I wasn't ready to see anyone just yet, not even Nefeli—as if I were waiting to first see Aris before anyone else, as if Aris was my link to the rest of the city. Eventually, though, I decided I should leave, if only to spend a little time outside the apartment before the sun disappeared. It was warmer outdoors than it was inside.

On the way home, I passed the tiny *periptero* across from my building. Not the usual free-standing kiosk, but a tiny storefront. Only one person could enter at a time, maybe two. "Myroula?" a voice called out to me, as if I were still my five-year-old self. I couldn't believe that Sophia, the Italian woman, still owned the little shop. Today she wore purple: purple jeans, purple sweater, purple velvet ballet slippers. Eyeshadow too—purple. She had owned the shop since before I was born.

She kissed me before holding me at arm's length so she could look at me. The last time I'd seen her must have been when I was in my twenties, visiting Haroula and Nefeli.

"I was so sad to hear," she said. "Memory eternal."

I nodded, thanked her. And because I wasn't sure what else to say, how to extricate myself from her sympathy, I bought some more chocolate, a few more bottles of beer.

"The Captain bought almost the same things," she said, handing me my change. "Plus cigarettes, of course." She looked past my shoulder toward our building, as if the Captain had just appeared. "So hysterical about smoking, Americans," she added, as if I both were and were not one of them. "You haven't met him?" Sophia asked. Almost an accusation.

"Not really." Not exactly a lie. He had not yet told me his name.

"A ship captain, though no longer working. He lived in America when he was young, too. Someplace cold, like you." Sophia shared everything and nothing. I remembered she had a key to our building, and probably most of the apartments in it, entrusted to her by the tenants. I had still not found the key to the building and realized I'd have to ask to borrow hers.

Sophia was now telling me the other things she knew about the Captain: that he was friendly but reserved, that though she'd known him for decades he talked very little of himself. He had two children, twins, though they were living with their mother abroad. She stopped speaking and watched my expression. "And you? Children?"

I shook my head.

"A pity," she said. "Why you girls wait so long," she added. I'd gotten nearly the same line from the taxi driver, who surveyed me through the rearview mirror to determine my age. "Well. You have time. *Me to kalo.*" I didn't have much time, if any, at all. I was already now referred to as "childless" as opposed to "without kids." I'd come to see that as we age, things are measured not in terms of potential but in terms of lack. And here, in Greece, to be a woman of a certain age without children, well. Perhaps this is why Nefeli and I were so close. We understood each other, the thing we never talked about but that bound us together.

My parents, my friends, even Aris: all of them thought I had postponed marriage and children for a career. But how could it be that simple? I liked my work fine. But an academic position, for me, was not my identity. It was my financial stability. I was proud to have just gotten tenure. But it was not my sense of self. What, exactly, was? That was the question.

The Captain, I was surprised to learn, had just returned from N., the island where my mother had inherited our place when I was ten, and it was where we'd return to when we came to Greece for the summer. My father always left after three weeks, but I'd stay through August with my mother, who, like me, was on an academic schedule. I had always felt bad for him, having to go back to work, but now I realize he enjoyed being in Chicago alone, temporarily freed from my mother's sadness.

"The Captain's father lives there," Sophia said, meaning the island. "You have a lot in common," she added.

She took me by the arm and led me outside, gesturing to the cigarette in her hand. We continued our conversation on the sidewalk while she smoked, and soon the Captain came around the corner, holding the newspaper and looking down at the ground.

Sophia looked my way as she blew a stream of smoke away from us, then nodded toward the Captain. "There he is."

*

I spent the rest of the evening drinking beer and rustling through the closets, which reached up to the high ceilings. There was far more here than I'd realized. I played old Greek records loudly on the old Victrola. I found a box of my baby clothes, as well as three more of Nefeli's paintings, lined up like books on a shelf. I hadn't seen these paintings before, figures of the same long-faced women but with their bodies erotically intertwined. In a little tin I found a bunch of orphaned keys. I threw some things away: a box of old rags; chipped mugs and dishes; some soft linens that smelled a little of mold; the baby clothes.

Excavating these remnants of the past, I felt neither nostalgia nor a particular connection. I felt newly empty. But when I tried to pinpoint the source of this haunting emptiness it was not clear.

Grief had become a part of me, like another layer of skin. But I think, now, I was grieving both the things that had happened and the things that would come.

One of the last boxes I opened held a collection of dolls dressed in intricate, traditional Greek costume. When I was a child these dolls had sat on my dresser, and at night I thought I saw their arms moving, their legs ready to march. They frightened me. Once I had taken several of them on a boat ride with my parents' friends. My parents, for all their love of the sea, were uneasy on boats, and my mother had been preoccupied with my falling overboard until she became too nauseated to worry. When no one was looking, I reached into my backpack and removed the dolls, which I'd fitted with parachutes made of my father's embroidered handkerchiefs noosed around their necks. One by one, I began to hurl them into the water. I must have thrown four of them out before my father noticed what I was doing and stopped me. After, the two of us watched them bobbing in the water, his embroidered handkerchiefs floating atop them, or spread out behind their heads. Still, these dolls seemed to be a common gift, continuing to accumulate over the years. There were at least a dozen of them lying haphazardly in the box. I returned them to the closet. It was too hard to discard something with a face.

2

The Captain

My mother was Greek American, and though that might mean my mother tongue is English, I was born in Athens and feel and dream in Greek idiom. But I'm not a man of geography. I don't attach myself to places. I'm more comfortable with the placeless universality of the sea, its altered progression of time.

Even though it's been years, I miss those long passages across the Pacific: the contained isolation, the morning rising up from the water like the opening of a shade, the creeping dread at the first sliver of land, like coming down from a high. How different the world looked from a point at sea. The sight of a harbor no longer stirs the same emptiness, but the sea no longer gives me that same unbridled joy. Everything seems dampened, my emotions less extreme, settling somewhere deep and less accessible. The true marker of middle age.

Katerina, my wife, has been working for the EU in Brussels since September, and the twins, because of my schedule at sea, have gone with her. At least, that was the reason we gave them for the arrangement. Nikos and Ifigenia, nine, don't know I'm no longer working. Katerina and I are separated, but we struggle with exactly what that means. We do not *not* enjoy each other's presence. There were times when we were younger that I raced home to see her, when the separations felt unbearable. Sometimes she'd even wait at the port. For me, these past years, it was not so difficult to be apart, but I imagine for her it sometimes was.

Not long after the move to Brussels last fall, Katerina's sister lost her job and had moved with her daughter into our home in Kifissia. We'd temporarily offered them the place. I was happy to live in the center of Athens anyway, in the apartment I've been in and out of my entire adult life. I've never liked the suburbs. And being in Kifissia—each time I say it, I hear my father's scorn, so *bourgeois*—felt as distant as being shipwrecked. We could have lived in Piraeus, or Glyfada, or Neo Faliro: somewhere near the port. But Katerina wanted to be near the kids' school.

So even after Katerina's sister moved out, having found work in Thessaloniki, I decided to stay in the Athens apartment. But now Katerina and the kids were coming home for the weekend— she'd promised the twins they wouldn't miss their best friend's birthday party—and I needed to be there, in the old house in Kifissia, as I was each time they returned.

Despite not being attached to places, I've grown fond of this Athens apartment. But those days there, waiting for Katerina and the kids to arrive, put me in a bizarre sort of limbo. I couldn't focus on any one task. I wandered the rooms, stood on the back balcony that looked out over the courtyard or the one in front, over the street, which curved up toward Lykavittos. The restlessness was overwhelming. The worst days for me, around transitions, are the days before. The waiting. Walking eased that torment a little, allowed me to move my body along with my racing mind. I walked through neighborhoods I'd rarely visited, into Kaisariani, its own village, really, with a history dating back to the Asia Minor refugees. I strolled the wide pedestrian walkway that wound around the Acropolis, watched the puppeteers and musicians, older tourists holding hands, American college students in tiny clothing. I walked through Psyrri, where the vibrancy of the crowded, lively cafés seemed to beat inside me along with my heart.

As for this apartment, it was the longest I'd spent here in years, and besides the sad-eyed woman whom I'd glimpsed in and out while the apartment was being renovated—a woman I later understood to be Mira's mother—I'd been alone on this floor. Even before Katerina and I had agreed to separate, I spent a night here every few months, those nights I had time off between routes but didn't want to sleep on the ship, didn't want to go all the way back home. To come home for a day sometimes seemed too disorienting for Katerina and the kids. Or so I told myself. Katerina and I both knew that it was simply disorienting for me.

One evening, I walked through the heart of Neapoli, where large concrete apartment blocks built during the junta transitioned to old neoclassical homes—some bright and well-kept, some in disrepair, many decorated with graffiti—and down the countless steps of Isavron, through Exarcheia, to Kallidromiou, where the breeze felt cool and airy. Here it was lively, the night pleasant, and under heat lamps people leaned in to intimate conversations, evening coffees, and drinks. I wore sweatpants and an old hooded sweatshirt, my indoor self turned outward, only my keys and phone and twenty euros zipped into my pocket. After wandering awhile, I climbed those steps again and reached Dexameni Square. Though it was too early in the season for the open-air cinema, the open-air café was packed: kids played on bicycles and pogo sticks, adults of all ages sat in large groups and small, drinking cocktails, eating *mezedes*. A couple my father's age—late seventies—sat on the same side of a table, glasses of white wine before them, holding hands and looking out, as if it were all theirs. The man wore a dark suit with a red cravat, and the woman's dark hair was perfectly styled, her dress navy blue with white piping, a trench coat draped over her shoulders. Their tranquil looks unsettled me, and I decided against sitting alone. Instead I kept walking until I reached one of my standby bars in Plateia Mavili, where I knew both the bartenders—a heavily tattooed bearded guy and a serious-faced young woman, whose ponytail swished back and forth as she worked. I drank a tall draft and headed home.

The walk back to my apartment was like strolling through a tiny village after a wrong turn, or something near the beach on a less-traveled island. Take any parallel street and you'd pass immaculate residencies with well-manicured gardens, yoga studios and law offices and trendy cafés. But on this route, a few chickens still hopped around, an old trailer was parked in the middle of a lot, and a fenced-in area held a mini junkyard: a few old cars, metal pipes, old furniture. There was only one actual house, and I loved it. It stood bright and cheery behind a rickety, makeshift fence, as if the concrete of the city had been built up around it, or as if I'd walked into a fairy tale. It looked recently restored: a warm, creamy yellow coat of paint, red tile roof, and a garden of bougainvillea and oleander and lemon trees. Next to it was an old shed, which had at one time needed a new coat of paint. Now, it had been painted with flowers and citrus trees, a mirror of its setting.

At home on my balcony, I smoked a cigarette. The courtyard was eerily quiet, and the night, with only a shaving of the moon, was dark. Only the sounds of the occasional motorbike, maybe a car radio. I slept a long, blank sleep until sunrise.

*

The next night Mira propped her feet on the balustrade, wearing sheepskin slippers. If the light was right you could see the shadow of a person behind the cloudy glass partition, and if we both leaned over the balustrade we could have had a conversation face to face. But we did not.

I had learned a bit about Mira from Sophia: she was from Chicago. A professor of some kind. Sophia wasn't sure. Her parents had recently died. Nefeli was her aunt. I thought of what I might say, if only in greeting. Then, the flick of a lighter, the inhale of a cigarette, the exhale of smoke. My words tumbled out before I could think. "I didn't know you smoked," I said. I had not only broken some unspoken code of communal living, I had implied a history. But if she found it odd she did not miss a beat.

"On and off. But I officially quit years ago, after college."

"I try to quit," I said, though I had stopped trying a few years ago. The couple who lived on the other side of the courtyard arrived home and began cooking, as they always did. Below them, someone made a video call in French, which happened every other night at eight. The neighborhood took on a new life in the evenings.

I asked if all was okay with the apartment, the heater.

She didn't speak at first, but her feet shifted. "I somehow lost the key to the building," she finally said.

There are three things you need to know about Greek apartment buildings, I told her. First, there's strong disagreement about whether to lock the front door, with the key, from the inside. So you also need a key to get out, after midnight. She said that sounded dangerous. I told her I'd be right back and I returned with my extra key, handing it across the balcony, and we met eyes for a moment, smiled. She thanked me and told me she'd make a copy. In the darkness her eyes seemed luminous and gray, as if in black-and-white film, and it took me a moment to focus on the rest of her, the contours of her body underneath a loose, dark sweater, a thin gold bracelet around her wrist and several woven from thread. Her dark hair was messy, wavy around her face.

It suddenly felt strange to be looking at her, so I retreated, sat back down in my chair. "Also, there's a fight over the elevator. The people on the first floor don't want to pay for it. The people on the second floor claim they don't use it. Finally, the question of how to heat the building, the most fraught of all."

She laughed. "Good to know." Her phone rang and she excused herself for a moment. "Hi, Dimitra," I heard her say as she disappeared inside. She returned moments later, telling me about a boy who was living with her friends Dimitra and Fady and their daughter, Leila. She mentioned a refugee squat nearby, in an old abandoned school, and asked me if I knew of it.

I told her I did not.

A silence hung in the space between us. I see now she must have misinterpreted my reticence, maybe took me to be a nationalist, xenophobic fascist. "You reminded me of something, of the time when I was still working, and the reasons now I'm not." My opportunity had come, and I could tell from the quiet that she was waiting for me to continue. But my words felt blocked.

"I understand," she said, finally. Though how could she. I excused myself and said goodnight.

*

The next morning, I picked up Katerina and the kids at the airport. The twins piled into the back seat as if I'd come for them after only a few days' absence, talking and planning for the birthday party that weekend. Katerina recounted the busy few weeks she'd had, something related to an upcoming funding deadline. As we turned onto our street, one of the more modest of the neighborhood, everything seemed larger and more open than I remembered. The trees seemed greener, the air crisper.

Between the car and the front door, Katerina and the twins were stopped by an eager neighbor. I steered around them, set the suitcases down, and took out my keys. When I opened the front door my chest tightened. The year had rewound—before I lost my job, before living full-time in the Athens apartment—but instead of feeling familiarity, I felt as though I'd stepped into another reality, another version of my life. As Rimbaud famously wrote: *I* is someone else.

The kids raced to their rooms to charge their devices, back to the house they knew as theirs. Katerina walked in, set the

23

groceries we'd stopped for on the counter. I began to unpack them, as was our custom, and she asked if I was still planning to accompany them to the island over the summer, when she'd take a couple of weeks off. She reminded me that as far as the kids knew, we were only separated because of work. I think Katerina and I often told ourselves the same untruth. There's a comfort in those things that remain unexpressed.

I reassured her that I planned to come to the island, and Katerina disappeared into the bedroom to take a nap. Ifigenia came out as I was finishing up with the groceries and sat on one of the bar stools in the kitchen, playing some internet game I did not understand, complaining about her brother. She wanted sympathy and some lemonade. With their mother, they helped themselves but when I was around they asked me for things. *Can I have some milk will you make me some cereal can you order souvlaki.*

There was a new refrigerator, sleek and chrome and tall, and I stood in front of it as though it were a portal. The old refrigerator had been fine. Not particularly old, even, just basic. There was also a new espresso machine, the kind that used not coffee but little pods, which didn't seem to me like coffee at all. All that pod-waste, drifting in the sea.

I stayed in the kitchen and read at the counter. Eventually, the twins must have fallen asleep as well because the house settled into quiet. The stillness of midday. I considered going outside for a cigarette. Katerina had always asked that we smoke outdoors, and the habit remained. After all these years I have come to prefer it. I like the ritual of stepping out of my space and into another, my balcony an urban observation deck. Even on the ship I smoked in the open air, never in my cabin, never enclosed.

But I decided to skip the cigarette and wandered down to the den, which was on the bottom floor and opened up to a small garden. I sat at the desk and opened the drawers, rifling through my things. I don't know what I was looking for. The domestic always made me restless, as if I were waiting for something to happen. After I was asked to leave the ship, I cleared out my cabin. One box was filled with little papers I had tacked up everywhere. Katerina found the notecards and Post-its and threw them away. I was enraged and went out to the dumpster in my bathrobe, trying to salvage them. "It was garbage!" Katerina said. She followed me outside. "Scraps of paper. There was nothing there." But there had been angst on her face.

It was odd, for Katerina had long ago stopped trying to clean out my things. There were things I gave up in marriage but there were things that I would not, and these artifacts now, more than ever, stood as a marker of my former self. Proof that he existed.

A few days after that, I had found several boxes wrapped on the bed. Katerina followed me into the room and smiled, told me to open them. "Happy Birthday," she said, almost shyly.

The first had held two athletic shirts, the kind that wicked away sweat, and a pair of basketball shorts. The second, a pair of expensive jeans she'd seen me glance at in an overpriced boutique. The third, though, held a leather-bound journal and a gorgeous pen. "I won't mistake this as garbage," she said, and I hugged her close.

*

We had carbonara, my favorite, for dinner. And perhaps because of the travel, the children grew tired soon after and went to sleep early. Katerina and I watched television together on the couch, a quiet closeness I'd forgotten I'd loved, until she announced she was exhausted and going to bed.

"I should call my father," I said. Katerina nodded. My father always expected me to come to him. I should call, I should visit, I should make the effort. It had been this way since I went back to the States for university. He was used to people coming to him: for political favors, for homage, for conversation and advice, like a mob boss.

I let the phone ring and ring, but no one answered. Finally I hung up, not wanting to wake him if he was already asleep. I would call in the morning.

I listened to Katerina in the bathroom getting ready, heard the water as she washed her face, brushed her teeth. I imagined her taking out her contacts, pulling her hair back. All the small rituals I knew so well. I waited until I heard the light click off before I went in myself.

But I paused in the doorway of our bedroom. I felt hesitant to get into the bed we'd shared for so many years.

"What is it?" Katerina asked, sensing me.

"Nothing," I said. "Should I sleep here?" I asked.

"Sure," she said. She was already under the covers.

I met Katerina when I was in my late thirties, and we married in my early forties, so there had been many women before her, mostly a series of relationships from which I always ended up fleeing. After we had the twins, I transitioned from sailing routes in the Pacific to ones in Europe, and while the change was difficult, the rhythm of my life on the Aegean was soothing in its own right. The inky-blue sea, the white froth of waves, the black dome of the nighttime sky opening each morning to each familiar port: small houses dotting the arid hillsides, scrubby patches of bright flowers, bleating goats. The landscape of my youth.

Though I switched to those shorter routes for my marriage, my family, Katerina would still argue that I'd missed the twins' most important years. And it's true; when I'd return home my kids eyed me bashfully, with interest—an intriguing, benevolent guest in their home. After being at sea, the skies in Kifissia had always seemed low, and the different schedule of my days as the twins grew—take them here, pick up some milk, help with the homework—though busy, felt featureless.

To Katerina I've been mostly faithful. Though I would never have thought this way as a younger man, now I think what so often drives people to infidelity is not sex but space. And because I was so often at sea I had space. Sometimes at sea I nearly forgot my other life, could almost not imagine it. What kind of man does this, forgets about his wife and children? I suppose I was that sort of man. My problem, one of them, was that I did not operate with the consciousness of a married person. I don't mean I went out at night like a wild bachelor, but I moved through space without thinking of the other person, without a deep awareness of that person at all times.

Katerina, however, did everything with a married person's consciousness, even now that we were separating. Or were trying to, anyway. Whether it was shopping for dinner or planning the kids' outings or simply the way she moved through the house— quietly in the morning when up before me, or reading at night in the other room if I wanted to go to sleep. I supposed you could only be in the world this way for so long without reciprocation before it wore on you; but it would take a while for her to adopt the consciousness of a single person, a single woman, a thought I found difficult to bear.

That night, I woke around three and our bed was empty, and for a moment I felt inexplicably angry. But I went into the kitchen and found Katerina barefoot in front of the refrigerator, a faraway look on her face. I wondered how long she'd been standing there.

"You okay?" I asked.

She turned to me but her expression remained vague, still colored by whatever, or whomever, she'd been thinking. Almost as if she did not recognize me, or had forgotten I was in the house. "Something to eat?" she asked. She lit the stove, reached up for the iron skillet, poured in some oil. When it was hot she dumped the leftover carbonara into the pan and cracked two more eggs over it, a dash of pepper, some nutmeg. We stood at the stove and ate it together, out of the pan, our bare feet touching.

3

Mira

That Aris wasn't in Athens when I'd first arrived did not seem ominous at the time, though when I think of him telling me he'd be back in a few days I feel a quick flash of dread, a weight inside me.

A few mornings after I'd arrived, Aris returned from Brussels. I repacked a suitcase, leaving much behind, and headed to his place. I had planned to spend the summer living with him and working on a collection of essays, a departure from my usual scholarly work. From the sidewalk, I looked up at Aris's building, the old neoclassical house where I had lived last summer and stayed many times before. I could see Aris on the balcony, but he wasn't looking down, waiting for me; instead he faced the inside of the apartment, looking in at something not visible from the street. I called to him, and though he knew I was on my way a look of surprise passed over his face, as if he didn't remember what I looked like, or what he was doing on that balcony in the first place.

But then he smiled, waved, and went inside to buzz me up. He met me at the landing and the moment I saw his face, of course, I knew something was wrong. In the corner of the apartment was the smaller shiny red suitcase I'd left last time. I did not yet know he'd filled it with all the things that had accumulated there over the years: books and clothing and a curling iron, several notebooks. When I see the pair of suitcases now in my own apartment, it's an obnoxious reminder of the humiliation I felt that day.

"It looks so nice in here," I said, moving through the flat, wheeling my suitcase behind me toward the bedroom. The place smelled lemony, freshly cleaned. The bathroom with fluffy white towels and the bed with light-blue sheets. Engagement gifts, though I didn't realize that until later.

It's when I stood in the doorway of the bedroom that he appeared behind me and put his hands on my shoulders. "Mira," he said. "We can't live here together." His voice was pained and tender but also that of a man who was expecting a fight.

It took me a minute to realize he wasn't saying he didn't want to live together but that he didn't want to be together at all. I don't remember how much he told me then and how much I'd learned after the fact. Another woman, it had happened so fast, he hadn't meant for it to become serious and now, he said, they were planning to marry. Her name was Eva.

Planning to marry. Also, she was having a baby.

I sat down on the bed.

"Mira. I couldn't tell you over the phone. It would have been cruel."

"When is she due?" I asked, looking down at the floor.

"Later this summer," he said.

So she had been already pregnant when my parents died. "You could have told me, in Chicago. Or in Athens, after the funeral."

"It felt inhumane. I'm sorry. There was never the right time." In a foggy state of shock I hauled both my suitcases back down to the landing—no elevators—refusing his help. Aris stood on the sidewalk with me and my bags, assuring me not *all* would change between us, that he still wanted me in his life. I got into a taxi, and I could feel him standing in the street, watching me drive away.

Later in the evening, a little drunk, I scrolled through my messages, not replying to anything. More texts from Aris—*Are you okay? Call me. Mira?*—as well as from Nefeli and my friends Dimitra and Fady. My father's cousins had called, but I didn't want to call them back. They had been anticipating an engagement, a wedding, and I didn't want to give them the smug satisfaction of knowing it wouldn't happen. They adored Aris, a handsome, hypereducated man with a new seat in parliament, but his involvement with me baffled them. They knew—because my mother had told them—that we both had imagined what our lives would be if I moved to Greece for good. Get tenure first, Aris had said. You'll be glad you did. And I was glad he felt this way, but when I did finally get tenure I felt no differently. It was not that I was that attached to teaching. Besides, so little of my job was teaching and so much was taken up with administration and meetings and navigating a department whose internecine struggles and alliances predated me. To be honest, I wavered between loving it and dreading it.

But perhaps Aris and I were both putting something off, or knew summers together, and Christmas, was enough, and maybe there wasn't anything wrong with that. But to my father's cousins it was not this complicated. To them I was not elegant enough, nor pedigreed enough, nor Greek enough; as if I had stolen him away from someone with better claims. I was their family, but I was not one of them.

Well. There would be *a* wedding. There was that.

Aris called again, several times, and finally I picked up.

"And she knows about me," I said.

"In the sense that you exist."

In the sense that I exist. I let him continue. *Do I exist.* I put him on speaker, set the phone on the table, needing the distance of his disembodied voice.

"That we had a history. I said your father was an old friend."

This was true. I'd met Aris three times before we really became involved: once, age eighteen, on the island, where I prowled around with friends from my freshman year; second, twenty-one, when I had a summer job bartending at an American bar on the island and he'd show up during my shifts, usually alone, and talk with me when I was not busy; and third, on the ferry, as a graduate student. This was the time that stuck. But he had loomed in my mind, my heart, since I was a teenager. He was part of me as I was forming, part of this place.

"That we were together, Aris. Can't you even say it?"

"Well, were we? *Really* together? Not since we both lived in Chicago. Not physically—not day in, day out."

"You're revising our history."

"That's what history is. Revision. Point of view. Of all people, you should know that."

It was the meanest thing he ever said to me.

"Mira?" he asked finally.

"I'm fine," I said. Aris wanted it to already be *after*, not understanding that the only way out is through. There was also the fact that he and my father had been particularly close. I understand that it would have been harder for Aris to leave me had my parents still been alive; once they were gone he had an escape.

"Would you even have wanted this?" he asked. "Marriage, a baby."

"Of course," I said, though neither of us completely believed me.

He was quiet, and he knew as well as I did that I had always resisted what was expected of me. Though I imagined marriage could be a beautiful thing, for me somehow it represented a sort of erasure. Couples often depressed me, and neat little families even more so. I don't know. Maybe I would have wanted it now, here, the different me in this different country.

The next morning, I called Nefeli and told her what had happened with Aris. I was dreading saying it out loud, as if saying it would make it true. But it was already true.

Half an hour later, she was at my door, telling me I looked terrible. She wore a black-and-white-striped T-shirt, jeans, boots, a red scarf wrapped stylishly around her neck. She didn't seem surprised. I could not block her out, nor could I hide anything from her. I returned to Athens each year and was seamlessly integrated back into her life, the rhythm of her days. What happened all those other months? I didn't know. We video chatted from time to time, but since my parents had died everything blurred together.

I asked her if she wanted a coffee, and she followed me into the kitchen, her eyes resting on the new countertops, the modern light fixtures, the empty bottle of wine on the dining room table, the paper bag of my finished beers and my mother's empties still on the floor. "What the hell," she said.

My head hurt.

I pretended not to notice the disarray—how often in the next few months I would willfully ignore something right in front of me—and poured us each a cup. "Don't drink so much, Myrto," she said. "Especially alone like this. It will only make things worse."

She held the warmth of the pale-blue mug close to her cheek for a few moments before she took a sip. She looked around at the sunny colors. "Haroula redid this?"

"My mother," I said, and her face showed some relief that it had not been Haroula who'd recreated the apartment, as if to rid it of Nefeli's presence. As a young girl I did not question the finer points of their relationship; they were simply Haroula and Nefeli. It was only after my freshman year in college, when I returned for the summer, that I finally knew them as lovers, partners, together. My parents had never explicitly mentioned their involvement but never denied it either. I suppose they might have been more socially progressive than I'd credited them for.

When I was a graduate student, in ethnographic studies, I read an anthropologist's study on women in same-sex

SCORPIONFISH

relationships in an unnamed Greek town. Many of them were
married to men, had children, and did not refer to themselves
as lesbian or queer. It might sound like they were victims of a
conservative society, certainly true, but there was a wonderful
progressive fluidity to it as a result: you can defy the system
if you refuse to let it define you. It struck a chord with me,
the freedom found between the lines and the way the women
had navigated conflicting identities, broke barriers. I found
myself deeply fascinated by these women, their nonchalance,
their structured freedom. I am not making the hetero mistake
of thinking that lesbian relationships are any easier than those
between anyone else. It was this particular group, unwilling to
declare one identity, that fascinated me. Was it oppression, or
freedom? What intrigued me most was the way relationships
were ended, the ritualistic collective grieving. How do you
say goodbye to a relationship? I had never been good at clean
breaks, old loves trailing behind me like shadows.

When we'd finished our coffees, Nefeli suggested we go to
the sea, which to her was the balm for everything. Though in my
opinion it was still too cold to swim, the sun was warm, and we'd
eat lunch by the water. She had been working hard preparing an
upcoming show, her biggest ever, and declared it would be good
to get out of Athens.

She followed me into the bedroom as I gathered a few things
for the beach. "Suffering is a chronic state," she said as I threw
things into a small bag. "I'm in this room with you, you see, and
I've got this gun. And I'm holding it above you, waving it around
your head, I'm chasing you around the room, and you're wondering if and when I'll shoot."

35

I didn't know then if she was talking about Aris or Greece, though later that summer, after she disappeared, I understood she'd been talking about herself. But Nefeli often spoke like a sibyl, and it had always seemed that she could sense things most others could not. I was also used to moments of deep joy with her: nights we'd laugh until we gasped for air, our stomachs aching. Just that morning, an old picture of us had popped up on social media, years earlier, the two of us drunk and laughing at a party on the island, me sitting on her lap at a crowded table.

She wandered out of the bedroom, and I heard the door to the apartment open as she headed into the foyer.

*

When we arrived, we dropped our things on the beach and took off our shoes. The sun felt marvelous. Usually Nefeli donned her goofy bathing cap and swam many laps back and forth, even when the weather seemed too cold. Today we both rolled up our jeans and shrieked as the water washed over our toes.

The day was bright, the sky a wild, changing blue. At the other end of the beach, a thin woman stood in a bathing suit and flippers, staring at the large rock in the distance, as if wondering what she was thinking in contemplating a swim. A bit farther down, at the end of the cove, was a beach chair nestled in the sand, a book atop it. Otherwise, we were alone. We walked through the scraggly beach grass up to the taverna that overlooked the sea. Light shimmered through the olive trees like an invitation to another world. We chose a table in the sun and ordered coffees.

Behind us sat a man alone, reading the paper. Across the terrace a blonde woman drank a frappé, while her two matching, curly headed children talked animatedly. She seemed genuinely happy. The man was cute, with faded jeans and a blue T-shirt. Brown hair messy from the beach, another cold-morning swimmer.

My phone lit up with two messages from Aris.

Nefeli glanced at it sitting between us. "This relationship will destroy you. Trust me."

"No longer a relationship," I said.

She looked at my phone. "I know Aris," she said. "He'll want it both ways."

Maybe that was true. Did I? Nefeli turned around to face the man behind us, and for a moment I thought she was going to ask his opinion. Instead, she asked for a cigarette, and when he leaned over to light it his eyes were on me. I smiled with closed lips. He offered me one but I declined. All this took place silently, in the span of a few seconds, but Nefeli caught it and rolled her eyes. He went back to his reading.

I looked out to the beach. The woman with flippers was now swimming toward the rock. Nefeli's words stung; less warning than accusation. She might be right. But perhaps *I* had been the one who'd wanted it both ways, who'd grown comfortable inhabiting, straddling, two worlds.

"Just be careful," she said.

I wanted to change the subject so I asked Nefeli about her upcoming show. She said it was bad luck to talk about it. I asked instead about her love life. A woman she'd been seeing was married to a man, which didn't work out too well; there was a woman

37

she liked in her tango class. "You'd think it would eventually go away, as the body changes. But no: desire is desire."

We walked back across the cool sand and arranged our blankets facing the water. I pulled my shirt off over my head and lay down on my stomach. Nefeli was telling me about spending more and more time on the island, even teaching a community art class in the big municipal building at the top of the hill, at the port. "Mostly British divorcées," she said. "Widows." Her soft chatter was comforting. And as she spoke, I was surprised by my eyes welling up. Nefeli paused. She placed her hand on the small of my back. "I'm sorry," she said. I closed my eyes and felt hot tears stream down my face. We stayed like this for a while, her hand offering me both comfort and permission. We didn't speak. I listened to the waves pile up against the beach, then recede, steady and reliable.

I dreamt of swimming, of my mother swaying on a boat, telling me to breathe: *One two three four five breathe.* When I woke an hour later, disoriented, Nefeli was still staring at the water. I glanced at her through half-closed lids, and for a moment I saw my mother, young, smooth skinned, embroidered dress, bottle of beer at her hip. *It's written on the body,* she said, or maybe it was Nefeli.

I rolled onto my side and Nefeli turned to me, noticing I was awake.

"Myrto, do you think I'll ever have sex again?"

I hoped the simultaneous surprise and relief in my face came off to her as amusement. "Definitely. Why wouldn't you?"

"I don't know. Eventually there is a last time, no?" She was quiet again. "He was looking at you, that man."

I laughed. "He was looking at my breasts." I couldn't tell if she was telling me to distract me, or to make me feel bad.

Nefeli's face changed then, kept her eyes focused on my chest. "Yeah," she said. "That's what I said." She paused, looked back out at the sea. A sailboat had appeared in the distance. "You should just chop them off. Get it over with."

Her tone was matter-of-fact but there was something else there, something that gave me the same hot wash of shame my mother could give in an instant.

I didn't know what to say, so I said nothing. Our relationship was tinged with something I'd never been able to name, something she occasionally threw in my face.

"Haroula wouldn't tell your family about me," she finally said. "We hid twenty years of our life together. Do you know what that does to you, to be hidden?" She raised her water bottle to her mouth, drank. She wiped her lips with the back of her hand.

"I can imagine," I said.

"I couldn't handle her shame. In my fifties there were others. And then I just got tired of people. All the shit they bring with them. I meet someone new and too quickly see the beast beneath.

"Among our friends it was fine. Artists. But when Haroula and I walked hand in hand in London, or in New York? So nonchalantly? I still cannot believe that was me. Never in Athens. Maybe it was just the freedom of travel. But I don't think so."

They'd been together, on and off, for eighteen years. Then Haroula moved to London, though she'd spent her last years back in Athens, in my apartment. But that was only the beginning of the end. Their relationship was a slow, painful fade.

"Most of my friends who are lesbian, queer, have always known," she continued. "Yet only half of them are out to their families. Maybe it's different now, for young people. I can see it.

But Greece is still a terrible place to be queer." She told me she'd had a quiet but vibrant community here, though after she and Haroula broke up she broke away from them. It was too painful. I nodded, keeping my gaze on the flat expanse of the sea. Somehow we'd never spoken of this before. "And your parents?"

"We fought over politics, not sex," she said. "How could we distinguish the two? How could we extricate identity from anything, from politics, from the art we make, the stories we tell, the things we feel? But I knew to drop it."

She pulled her beach bag onto her lap and began rooting around for something. "People become uncomfortable when you can't be pinpointed. Ambiguity makes people nervous. I've had two loves of my life, very different. One was when I was very young. It was also something we kept hidden. He was married." She looked up at me to see my reaction.

"Not judging."

"We were in a camp together during the junta." Nefeli pulled out a little metal cigarette case painted with a watercolor of the Eiffel Tower. Inside were several tightly rolled joints and a pale-green lighter. She lit one of the joints, took a long drag, and then continued. "I loved this man, also an artist. It was mostly emotional anyway. Chaste. I was confused then; I didn't understand my own sexuality. But it didn't matter: he walked off the boat into the arms of his wife, the first I'd known of her. I remember her trench coat, her open, happy face, and I knew I never again wanted to be a ridiculous girl."

Even though I had not known her then, Nefeli was easy to imagine as a teenager: the wide, amber-colored eyes, her hair still long and shiny and black. She continued: "He loved me like a little pet you take care of. You know what can happen to women in those camps. And when we returned, when the junta was over, he asked Nikos"—she paused, in case I hadn't yet made the connection, though I just had—"the Captain's father, to look after me. For years, I think he bought my paintings, instructed by this man. Eventually I think he gave them to Haroula."

Nefeli stubbed out the rest of the joint, put what was left back in the small metal tin. "The body and mind are the same thing," she said. I suggested lunch. We walked back to the taverna and sat at a table half in the sun, for me, and the shade, for Nefeli. Both the blonde woman with the kids and the handsome man were gone. Now, a table of sunburned tourists drank beers from frozen mugs.

We sat there a long time, ordering first a salad and then some fried zucchini that only I ate, and some fava. Nefeli didn't eat meat and refused to sit with others if they did. We shared a beer and then another. Eventually she got up to use the bathroom, and when she returned she declared she had paid the bill, that she was tired and wanted to leave.

Nefeli immediately fell asleep as I drove, but after twenty minutes she awoke. We were nearing the center. The traffic was terrible. A strike, a protest, a 5K run—Nefeli wasn't sure. "You know which two countries report the highest levels of stress?" she asked, staring out the window. I glanced at her so she'd go on, and she turned to me. "Greece and Iran." She let out a deep breath.

The road felt like an enormous parking lot. Young men wandered between the stopped vehicles, dangled gadgets and toys in front of windshields, a captive audience in the gridlock, and I was surprised when Nefeli handed the man a couple of euros for a little wind-up toy.

After an hour we reached Nefeli's, and I parked her car in the lot below her building. We each got out and hugged goodbye, but she hesitated before taking the elevator up. "I need to show this to you," she said, scrolling through her phone. "I'm sorry I waited this long."

I was hoping it had to do with her new work, something from her show. But it was an online magazine, and not even one of the more horrible ones, basically hypothesizing Aris and Eva as a couple. Eva was a fairly well-known actress, Greek French. In the past she'd done mostly smaller, artful movies, often French, but a new international hit with a Greek director had catapulted her into the spotlight. And Aris, after all, was a rising politician. They were both attractive and intelligent, and the Greek newspapers ate this up. I couldn't bear to read it and handed Nefeli back her phone. "I'm sure these sorts of things are everywhere."

"Scroll down."

I did and was startled by my younger self, smiling like an idiot, walking up a marbled, narrow island street. It was more than a decade ago; I don't think I was even thirty. I wore cut-off jeans and a blue bikini and held an ice cream cone—who knows where they'd unearthed this photo. The picture was juxtaposed with a horribly unflattering shot of Eva smoking a cigarette, looking angry. I had seen her in movies years before and knew she was beautiful, but the photo unfairly depicted a tired, too-thin actress who was not aging well.

Until, of course, the love of a man could change that: the next photo told a different story, the two of them together, each looking impossibly youthful. Eva had a deep intelligence in her eyes.

Aris was smiling big, looking at something out of the picture, and Eva was looking up at him. When was this taken?

"I'm glad you showed me." Of course I felt sick.

"You're lying," she said. "But in case someone else brought it up."

"Who else reads this nonsense?" I asked. I was furious at the stupid magazine. It might as well have read, *Upcoming politician rejects well-fed American and transforms aging, starving Greek actress.*

Aris had stayed with me those two weeks after my parents' death, in Chicago, helping me clean out their things. From there we made arrangements about where in Athens they would be buried. He tossed cardboard boxes of old magazines into recycling bins as if he were shooting baskets, and we made a race of how much we could discard in the shortest amount of time. I ran in and out of the house in a frenzy, but when I found the boxes of my father's old records, I crumpled into Aris's chest, and we didn't do any more with the dumpster that night. I'm trying to reconcile those tender moments with the fact that already, at that time, he was with Eva. The worst part of a betrayal is trying to reconstruct the events around it: what you knew then and what you know now. But I have to believe his tenderness then was sincere and not simply a manifestation of his guilt, of the fact that his second narrative was occurring simultaneously. I know human relationships are complex and multilayered and fluid, that it is possible to feel things for more than one person, to want two opposing things. Eventually, you have to choose.

Still, it didn't make it any easier to handle.

But besides the shame of Aris's other romantic narrative, I felt spied upon retrospectively, as if something had been taken from me without my knowing it. Even in our tell-all, display-all world, I use social media sporadically. The few photos circulating of me have been posted not by me but by friends. Perhaps it's the dissonance that's too much, the fragments that never make a whole: here I am in a bikini on the beach, here I am with a glass of wine and a big grin, here I am giving a lecture, here I am by the sea.

I told Nefeli I'd see her that weekend, at Fady and Dimitra's. Then I turned and headed down the sidewalk toward my apartment.

I admit that I don't always see the things people say about Athens—it's dirty, it's chaotic. Sometimes I'm not even sure what people are talking about. It's a city. There's traffic. If anything, people are always sweeping the sidewalks and washing the staircases. But after the sea that day, the freshness of the breakup and the sting of those photos, Athens felt like an assault, like all its violations were announcing themselves to me, questioning my decision to be there—the traffic stopped everywhere and people honking their horns, frustrated in their cars. Every car, it seemed, confined couples and lovers bickering over the route not taken; or sitting silently, the passenger staring at their phone and the driver at something ahead they could not see. I noticed all the boarded-up buildings, the closed businesses. I ducked down a side street and passed a young man in a blue-and-black flannel shirt rolling up his sleeve, his other friend watching, waiting. Sure, you might have run into a person strung out near Omonia, wandering around the Archaeological Museum, far before this new crisis. I distinctly remember Haroula telling me, when I was eighteen, in English, as if this could not be uttered in Greek: *watch out for junkies.* Yet unless I was in a particular neighborhood at night, I never really noticed, but Nefeli, who seemed to absorb the shame of the entire nation, claimed people shot heroin on the streets the way Americans walked around with their giant cups of coffee. If my American friends had said something like this I would have bitten off their heads.

And wouldn't this be the same in any city? But I admit, it was jarring against the backdrop of those grand neoclassical buildings, that architectural trilogy. And I admit I had my blind spots with this city, a city people either Orientalized or romanticized, two versions of the same sin. Even though it was the city of my birth, perhaps because of it, I was surely guilty of both. There's no such thing as perfect vision, true, but how to rid oneself of blindness?

As I walked through the last of the traffic I was relieved to be walking alone, moving freely between the cars, up the sidewalks, through the park, and up along the side of Lykavittos, spared most of the mess.

*

Back at home, I went to my balcony. I think I was hoping to find the Captain, but his apartment was quiet. Around ten, I heard his key in the door and soon after I smelled cigarette smoke. I stepped out onto the balcony and waited until he registered my presence. A shift in his seat, a change in the air. *Kalispera,* Captain.

He returned the greeting. I heard the ice clink in his glass.

When I was a child my mother would pour her first drink immediately after her classes. She'd make me dinner and pick at something herself. My friends' family dinners were an endless source of fascination. Mothers who ate at the table! Or my best friend's mother, who always washed dishes while her husband and four girls ate; another lived only with her mother and brother, and after school her brother made us chocolate chip pancakes for dinner as he drank beer from a can. He was seventeen, usually shirtless. I loved him deeply.

"Were you close with your mother?" I asked.

"Very," the Captain said, as if the forwardness of my question were routine, as if we'd always spoken this way.

"I'm fascinated by people's mothers. But I was most comfortable in the houses where they felt invisible," I said. "Or crazy." As a young girl I had had the sense that it was my duty to take care of my mother, not the other way around.

I heard the Captain exhale. Shift in his chair.

I continued:

"The nights my father was gone, playing bouzouki in Greektown, my mother watched television in the den and drank. Sometimes I confused her cries with those that came from *ER* on television. I would wander from my room, where I talked on my princess telephone to friends, and stand at the door like a sentry. Sometimes she realized I was there and the cries stopped, the bad dreams. Maybe drunken hallucinations. I don't know. When my mother began sleeping in that room for good I told my child-self that she liked the television, which my father did not."

Even then I had known the power and comfort of a good, solid lie.

"Those nights, when she stopped the bizarre mix of conversation and terror-stricken cries she'd have with herself, I was released from my duty. But I never went back to my bedroom.

46

I'd fall asleep in the high-ceilinged living room, watching televi-sion—*Saturday Night Live* or a movie or those ridiculous night-time soaps that I stupidly loved. In that large room I felt safe on the couch but terrified to move, to pass the den door, afraid my mother would stir from her drunkenness and say something un-intelligible or mean. So I'd remain on the couch until my father returned from his nightclub and carried me up to my room."

The smell of tobacco in his shirt pocket had signaled that I was off duty and could collapse into childhood again.

"My mother never got over leaving Greece," I said. "She left for my father." I know now my mother's excitement for a new life, those last days in Athens, had been a manic state of denial. "Each visit back was painful to her, yet being away was even worse."

"The scourge of the exile," the Captain said. "Not being able to forget."

"My mother existed in two places but lived nowhere, whereas my father existed in two places and lived everywhere." I am sure my mother had moments of happiness in Chicago, but I don't remember them. The closest I could remember was when she puttered around in her small rock garden in our yard, or sat in the early autumn sun, reading. On the island, things felt a little better, but I think she was always thinking of the moment she'd have to leave.

The Captain didn't say anything, but I could feel him listen-ing, as if he'd been listening to me for years. He did not ask many questions, and I liked him for this. It was not aloofness or disin-terest. Something else. A sense of space, not distance. It occurred to me right at that moment that everything with my mother had been performance. But pain all the same.

My parents, and me by proxy, were not always aware of two worlds but always aware of themselves from the perspective of the other one. It seemed that the traits of my personality were always viewed as a product of my Americanness, not my Miraness. For instance, I was nearly always on time. My parents' sense of time, which I do not attribute to their Greekness but to something else, infuriated me as a child. I was late to school plays, to school, to birthday parties; I was often the last to be picked up. My father would begin lathering his face to shave at the time they were supposed to be at a dinner.

"What time is it there?" my parents would ask a relative when they spoke, as if the rules for time elsewhere moved forward at their own accord, that those eight hours were as arbitrary and changeable as my mother's moods. The only time they kept sacred was the evening weather report, before which my father would angrily hush any conversation or noise, as if our quiet obedience would ensure the early arrival of spring, and the nightly Lucky Lotto drawings broadcast on WGN.

But their dual identities were clear. When in Greece, they saw things through American eyes, and when in America, through Greek eyes. My father flourished like this. He loved it, he fed off it, he became a larger version of himself. But my mother, I think it slowly killed her. She was displaced in Chicago, and when she was back in Greece she felt a more acute, sad kind of displacement. She didn't exist fully formed in either place, and she slowly melted away.

Had I said all this out loud, or to myself? I was suddenly sleepy, but when I said goodnight to the Captain and fell into bed, sleep would not come. The bed felt hard, and I tossed and turned, my eyes wide open. But I must have slept eventually because I woke to the sounds of a woman's screams. First I lay there, unsure if I was dreaming. I suppose I'm still not certain—there is a small chance it was a dream, and for many consecutive nights in that apartment I'd awake completely confused. But even as I say as much, I feel my guilty conscience: I could no longer blame the disorientation of jet lag, or even a new space. And because of this I cannot shake the feeling of shame that accompanies this confession: lying in bed, unable to even move my arm to reach for the phone, sheer terror surrounded me as a woman screamed for help. I could have immediately dialed the police, I could have gone out to the balcony and called to her. Maybe even if I had made my presence known, the assailant would have run. Maybe she was with a lover, an episode of violence unfolding right in front of their home.

Her screams for help were clear and deliberate. *Voítheia.* Help. And they became more frantic, more terrified, more muffled. They were from a living body, they were not my imagination, but I could not move.

Finally, the silence released my limbs and I was able to tear myself out of the bed and onto the balcony. I called the police and explained to them where I was. I called out to her.

But I was too late. The night had swallowed her up.

The next night, I asked the Captain about the screams. Though he slept with his balcony doors open, he said he had not heard a thing. The ship made him a light sleeper, he added. Always ready for an emergency.

"You really heard nothing?" I asked.

"Not even the cats," he said.

I wasn't sure where the screams were coming from. Lykavittos? Near the stadium? Sometimes what sounded like music from a party in the next building was coming from the park that was a fifteen-minute walk away. But I know these are excuses that I make because of the helpless shame of lying in my bed, my shoulders pinned down by fear.

"Are you okay?" he asked, finally. "Mira?"

I realized sleep had taken hold in the chair and I'd been dreaming of driving around with large green-and-turquoise sea charts I could not read, trying to place one into my eye like a giant contact lens. I told him this.

He laughed, a deep, gentle laugh. "You remind me that I haven't paid attention to my dreams. I'm probably having them but my sleep has felt blank."

"That sounds wonderful. I'm often teaching in my dreams, about to lecture on a subject I know nothing about."

He was quiet. I wasn't used to talking to someone who didn't interrupt each sentence. I continued. "Except suddenly I'm bartending, my boss complaining about the wrong drink, words spilling out of her glass, across the television screens while I fumble with a tiny lock on luggage, or try to dial a phone number."

"Me, driving a car into the water and sinking; or worse, watching my kids drown and not being able to help them. Of water, of blindness, of rock."

I was quiet, trying to imagine his kids. Twins.

"I've never told that to anyone," he said.

"Terrifying." The woman and her scream came back to me. But it had not been a dream. "So hard to explain." I paused. "'A dream cannot exist in words.'"

"Is that—"

"From *Maria Nephele*," I said.

"Elytis." He seemed disappointed. Elytis bored him, he said. The sun, the sea, we get it. He spoke a bit more but I felt drowsy, suddenly sleepy.

Later, I woke draped with a white blanket that was not mine and a vague image of him handing the blanket to me, a quick glimpse of his face. I rose from my chair, went inside, and flopped down onto my bed, feeling an odd rush of euphoria.

4

Mira

The next evening I went to Fady and Dimitra's for dinner. When I arrived at their place, Fady shouted down the staircase excitedly as he heard me walking up, and when I appeared on the landing he threw his hands into the air. He was wearing an apron printed with blue fish, holding a wooden spoon.

"Cute outfit," I said, and he and Dimitra pulled me in close for kisses and a hug.

"I never liked him anyway," Fady whispered. I laughed, knowing that of course he had liked Aris; they were friends, but there was a tenderness in the comment. Dimitra never quite trusted him, didn't find him believable—another neoliberal in a leather jacket pretending to be a progressive—and I didn't feel like arguing about something I had lost faith in myself. What Aris wanted, Dimitra posited, was for people he didn't know to adore him. Nefeli, on the other hand, had simply tolerated him, having known him since he was a petulant child. Aris and Nefeli had always approached each other with a slightly proprietary arrogance, and I long ago had given up trying to have them be friends.

I handed Dimitra a bottle of wine, some flowers. She set them down and took both of my hands, looking into my eyes a long time, as if trying to say something. She had big honey-colored curls and a contrasting cool demeanor; she loved wine and was able to turn anything into a brainy conversation. When they welcomed me in, I made my way around the boxes that jam-packed the foyer. Dimitra told me they were Arabic-language books for the refugee camps and the various squats in Athens.

If my parents were my connection to a nostalgic Athens, and Aris to an ideal one, then Nefeli and Fady and Dimitra were my connection to the present moment, a guide to a reality of this city that, as the American journalist Kevin Andrews had written decades earlier, was both the most intense and the least visible. I had known them all for years. Though Fady was a violin maker by craft, he also worked as an interpreter, with his connections to both speakers of Arabic and Dari. Fady has lived in Athens since he was in his twenties. His small workshop, which he used to live and work in, is at Plateia Mavili. If we wanted, Dimitra often joked, we could throw Molotov cocktails from his workshop balcony to the US embassy.

When I spoke to Dimitra earlier, she had told me Fady was out, taking a Syrian family to the asylum office, and about the absurd system they'd had to navigate to get the appointment. She told me about unaccompanied minors, refugee kids selling themselves in the park. A father with toddlers, his wife who had made it with their infant girl to Germany. Two separate boats, one stopped by authorities, one let go. The blurring lines: the volunteer agencies doing more than the NGOs, the journalists becoming volunteers, the refugees themselves organizing better than any government agency—at least the ones in Athens, not those isolated in festering, overcrowded camps on the peripheries.

While everyone else in Athens was struggling financially, Fady and Dimitra squeaked by. They'd been better off years before, of course, but they were still afloat. By Greek standards, anyway. Fady's hypothesis: If people had money they were investing in expensive things like instruments, and a lot of his business came from the better-off countries of Europe. They lived in a bizarrely large flat for an even more bizarrely low rent on the border of Neapoli and Exarcheia, about a ten-minute walk from my place. Dimitra also owned a small but gleaming apartment in the center that she rented on Airbnb for three times the price of their own. A necessary evil, she said, knowing the way it drove rents up. The taxes on it, in addition, were terrible.

Fady hated idleness: he was either building a cello or restringing a violin or working as a freelance interpreter. He was incredibly skilled at video editing and worked with friends on a documentary; he was friends with the Balinese graffiti artist and the Greek Argentinian singer and the aging, slightly deranged leftist composer. He knew everyone. His hobby of sound art was becoming a second career. He and Nefeli were working together on her new installation, part of her upcoming show, though I didn't yet know its details. My point: You would never call Fady and find him binge-watching a television series or sucked into social media. Dimitra was a freelance journalist and a gorgeous singer. When up for it, she sang in a few little bars across the city.

People often came to Dimitra and Fady when going through a tough time—just last month they'd had two friends, journalists from Ankara who no longer felt safe there, staying in the guest bedroom. They helped them settle in Athens, and when Dimitra told me the story, introduced us, I recalled the way she and Fady, and a tiny Leila, had taken me to the new IKEA to make sure I had a proper desk, a comfortable living space, in that small flat I'd rented in Pangrati as a grad student. Leila still had the stuffed giraffe I'd bought for her then, flopped over her dresser. Days later, when I had attempted to build the desk, filled with white-hot rage as I stared at a diagram instructing me to get onto a diving board, Dimitra came over and we put it together within an hour. Being with them always calmed me down.

"Nefeli's not with you?" Dimitra asked, going back to the door, which was still open, peering into the stairwell, as if she were about to tell me a secret. I, too, wanted to tell her about that strange afternoon at the sea, but the doorbell rang and they buzzed her up. When Nefeli reached the landing and smiled, looking refreshed and rested, I relaxed.

The traffic and commotion of our arrival summoned Leila. It had been two years since I'd seen her, and I almost did not recognize the teenager before me: her dark, shiny hair piled messily high atop her head, black leggings, black T-shirt, black-rimmed glasses like Fady's, black Ugg boots. When she was younger, she would come flying around the corner and throw herself onto me for a hug, her arms wrapped around my waist. She'd lost her youthful gregariousness and now shared Dimitra's unnerving demeanor, which on a near-child was almost disarming.

But I insisted on a hug and she stepped toward my open arms. Pulling her toward me, I spotted a younger boy—though at this age it was hard to tell—standing in the space she'd just occupied, and I knew this must be Rami. Rami had arrived last fall, alone, from Damascus; his father and Fady had been childhood friends, and he'd managed to make it to Athens and reach them there. He should have been in a Greek school by now, but some snafu with paperwork, with the bureaucratic maze, had delayed his enrollment. Dimitra had told me he wanted to be a writer and had asked, over the phone, if I'd consider tutoring him. I'd happily agreed. Rami had relatives in Germany, an uncle and aunt and cousins whom he missed dearly, and an older brother too, who'd taken it upon himself to leave first. When they'd left, Rami's parents had still been alive. As I understood it, unaccompanied minors were able to apply for reunification with family elsewhere. Yet ushering this long and arduous process along was another story, and it seemed the rules were always changing. And so he waited. I knew Dimitra and Fady loved him deeply, said they'd be happy to have him stay forever, but it was complicated; Rami's aunt—his father's cousin—and Rami's brother were already waiting for him in Berlin.

In the meantime, Rami had spent two months at the American school with Leila; the teacher was a friend of Dimitra's and had looked the other way. But when some of the parents found out he wasn't officially registered they threw a fit.

So aggressively denying one child, can you imagine?

I released Leila and as she withdrew from my embrace she caught my gaze.

"My cousin," Leila said warmly, gesturing toward the boy, though I knew not actually. Rami smiled shyly and nodded, then he and Leila scampered back into the den to continue their game, children again. Fady called after them in Arabic, and Dimitra in Greek, and Leila called back, "I know I know," in English.

This had been the linguistic landscape of my childhood neighborhood in Chicago: those first- or second-generation tri-lingual households of likely and unlikely combinations, children toggling between languages without hesitation. But Leila would be one of those international, cosmopolitan kids I'd known in college, global citizens more than anything else. I had not been this way; I had been only an immigrant, there was nothing cosmopolitan about my experience, and if there had been it was by mistake.

Dimitra mentioned that a friend of hers, an acquaintance of mine, had seen me in the cheese shop in my neighborhood. He wasn't sure if it was me so he didn't say hello, but this rattled me. For some reason I had been moving through Athens with the sense that I was invisible, that somehow, without Aris, without my parents, I had lost the definition of my physical self. That I was somehow deconstructing and recomposing myself all at once.

I never imagined I'd allow a man, or any relationship, to de-fine me, yet I'd allowed it to happen anyway. I'd told this to Fady once, and he had shrugged and said, "But why not? What's wrong with being defined by love?"

As the dinner neared its conclusion, we decided to skip the dessert, some tiny cheesecakes Nefeli had brought from the sweet shop, and head to the nearby bar where Dimitra would sing. Ta-ble cleared, we gathered coats and shoes to leave. I watched Fady pull on a quilted down jacket, as if we were in Chicago. "What?" he said, laughing. We walked out, my *parea* dressed for snow and

I for the beach. Yet when I wrapped my cardigan close around me, Nefeli caught me: "You see?" she said, laughing, and pulled an extra scarf for me from her bag like a magician.

Dimitra was the singer but it was Nefeli who began belting out Kazantzidis as we strolled outside, before we'd even reached the bar. "Life has two doors," she sang, and this—along with the abundant wine we'd already drunk, despite the pain of the song— put us all in a one of those open moods, a heightened emotional state. Rami and Leila, who'd disappeared as soon as they'd finished eating, peered down from the balcony and watched with amusement, as if we adults were a spectacle of entertainment. Nefeli stretched her arms out and moved in a circle, and Leila and Rami, with smirking irony, began to clap for her from above. But me, I felt so full of raw emotion and pain and sadness I could have burst. Later, when Nefeli was gone, I tried to remember her at that moment. Watching her sing this song as if her life depended on it, I could have ripped my heart from my chest and flung it to the ground as if it were a plate.

*

The bar was small and cozy, the walls painted orange and red, the bar and its stools a deep golden yellow. Small black tables and chairs, with an eclectic mix of glasses and plates, as if everyone in the bar had raided their yiayia's china cabinets to assemble the tableware. The wall that faced the street was made of windows, drawn open onto the outdoor patio that was dotted with heat lamps. We sat inside, closest to the windows and the musicians. Dimitra's speaking voice was rather low, but her singing voice had an impressive range: clear and feminine and sonorous, with a striking degree of pain. A female Kazantzidis, Fady always said. He, like Kazantzidis, considered Western music rootless. Jazz? Dimitra would ask him. Blues? He remained unconvinced. "You make violins, Fady," she'd say. But it was Dimitra who was the purist, and Fady'd fallen in love with Greek music—all of it, Kazantzidis especially, with his focus on *xenitia* and exile, loss— when he fell in love with Dimitra at university years ago.

A strange comparison, maybe, but you'd understand the moment Dimitra parted her lips. A clear, intense depth, like water you could look deep into and see your feet, the urchins below, the small details on the fish swimming by.

I watched the bouzouki player, only half our age but playing like my father had, his cigarette held between his pinky and ring finger, and I could feel the hot familiar swell of anxiety in my chest. Dimitra had little patience for anything even relatively new. She and my father were similar that way. But beyond his aversions and his predilections—Greek coffee, early morning walks, elegant wool sweaters, old *rebetika*—I had hardly known the man at all. I know he had had deep pain, that the pain of exile for him was so intense that he suppressed it entirely. It was why Greek music made him so emotional, made him weep.

But I don't mean to sentimentalize him. We are harder on mothers than on fathers, who simply need to show up once in a while, cook us an egg. My father used to call me when I was in college, early, always on the landline—how strange now, a landline, though I had one here in this apartment—to see if I was awake and sleeping at home. He timed it just right: too early for me to already be out for class, but late enough to make sure I was not sleeping in. Seven-thirty a.m., on his way to work. It didn't matter if I was out until two studying, or at a party, or when I had worked at a bar and didn't return home until three or four in the morning. He believed in what he called "normal" hours, and anything else was a sign of weakness, laziness, or defeat.

And he was hard on me. A 97 percent had him asking for the other three points, and when he was angry at me he could give me the silent treatment to end all silent treatments. But he was also, as they say, a *hazobabas*. He spoiled me.

Fady was asking something I didn't hear. He was a good man, warm and reliable and generous, and Dimitra and Fady's relationship always impressed me. They balanced one another; Dimitra always cool yet wildly spontaneous, and Fady more warm and open but with a measured accuracy to his behavior. Despite the years together, two decades, it was fresh, energetic, not bogged down by suburban lethargy or middle-age malaise. Leila became a part of their life, integrated in, as opposed to her becoming what their life revolved around. Make no mistake, though: Fady was besotted with his little girl, and now with Rami too, the three of them shooting baskets in the evenings in the park around the corner, or going to the Saturday market together to decide what to cook. They were fluid in that way, always open for something new.

Though I saw it as the ideal, I couldn't bring myself to attempt it; I'm more comfortable as a guest outside the family unit then as a member of it. Or maybe I craved a more capacious definition of family. Fady said my name again.

Next to us, a table of drunk and beautiful young actors from the National Theater sang along with Dimitra's version of *Trele*

Tsigane, one of my favorites. Nefeli sat up in her chair, alert, and she touched Fady's hand.

Then I turned to the street and there was Aris. He was walking past us, in a group. What was he doing in this neighborhood? We had come here together in the past, to this bar to hear Dimitra sing, and to the taverna next door, but lately he preferred posher neighborhoods, less fraught with political agitation. I downed my drink and reached for the little pitcher of raki.

I wanted to stand—partly to verify that it was truly him, and partly to mark this territory as mine after finally being able to imagine myself doing so—but I forced myself to sit through the rest of the song. When the musicians took a break, however, I left Fady and Nefeli and Dimitra talking with some others and excused myself to the restroom. My curiosity was bold and drunk and I found myself, stupidly, marching to the taverna. Sam, our usual waiter—a tall, cute, Eritrean guy—smiled and pointed to the table in the back, where I usually sat with my friends and where Aris now sat with his group.

That's when Aris looked up. I tried to catch a glimpse of Eva, how could I not, looking as I'd remembered her from movies. Long wavy hair, blonde highlights, large hoop earrings, red lipstick. Then I caught the eye of one of her friends—blue blouse, hair piled atop her head, dramatic dark eyebrows arched, alert. A parade of women marched through my mind, women who'd blatantly flirt with Aris at this or that event, me by his side. Had Eva been one of them?

Then a man raised his hand, a solid, unmoving wave. The Captain. All this made it all the more disorienting, and Aris probably saw that in my face. Looking terrified, Aris gestured for me to wait as I turned and walked back out to the street, where he soon caught up with me. I led us into the small alley behind the taverna. Aris took both my hands in his, in what first seemed a gesture of affection but that I quickly realized was one of restraint.

If I thought I had detected some anguish at his first glance, I was wrong; the fear on his face that I'd make a scene shot rage and shame through me. But when have I been the type of woman to make a scene? My mother had made scenes, spontaneous outbursts in department stores, inexplicable road rage, irrational anger about a mistake on a phone bill or a bank statement, drunken displays at parties or just from the front porch.

He let go of my hands. I had once loved the way he'd looked at me, but over the past few years his gaze had begun to feel slightly more judgmental than appreciative: his awareness of what I wore, how smoothly I styled my hair, was my dress right, became my awareness too. It's not that he was critical, but I was certainly scrutinized. Or maybe it was my perception of his gaze that changed. Our breakup thrust me into an Athens I now navigated in my jeans and boots and sweaters, free of any sort of false trappings, makeup, any sort of disingenuous performance. The breakup, the online photos: they all felt abstract. But seeing them—him and Eva—out together, another night with friends: that was when it hit.

The din from the taverna seemed louder, more boisterous. People milled around the street now, smoking, some in front of the bar where Dimitra was singing. I could hear her going into another of my favorites. Down the middle of the street a group of teenagers walked by, dressed in torn black clothing, followed by a group of German tourists, mostly women in their sixties in colorful T-shirts, taking the teens' photo from behind.

I moved to go past him, but he grabbed my arm. I didn't want to talk and I certainly didn't want to argue. What did I want, then? A fresh wave of shame washed over me, the thought of him wandering this neighborhood hand in hand with his fiancée. I wanted to see it, to go back into the taverna and get a good look at them together. I wanted the sting of it. Hell, I wanted to watch her in their house, taking a shower, fucking Aris in his bed, having an orgasm on the kitchen counter, her expensive heels falling to the floor as she curled her toes. I wanted to watch him touch her body. I wanted to see. What she had, what she was. What I wasn't.

I was sick; I was losing the plot, but for a moment that's what I wanted.

"Mira," he said.

"You hate this neighborhood," I said.

Eventually we'd cross paths. I was still close with his father; we both visited the island regularly. Yet if Aris was thinking this, he didn't have the cruelty to say it.

"I didn't—" he began, but didn't finish. "This isn't easy for me," he said.

It is impossible to piece together where something went wrong when all we have are memories, and memories of memories. You could take them all and line them up, each moment, but it would never add up to a life. What makes a life is the white space, the glue that holds everything together. It is impossible to know, impossible to understand. I had thought everything lay in the unsaid.

I couldn't look at him. "What exactly do you want me to say? You want my *blessing*, for fuck's sake?"

"You know how much you mean to me," he said. "Always."

"But you love her," I said. For years I had simply assumed, projected, that because I felt that invisible line linking us, no matter what, that he did too. I was dizzy. Affection and love are not the same thing.

"It's not only about love," he said. "You're simplifying."

"I don't know. I think it is," I said.

I felt like I had woken up from a deep sleep unsettled, confused, trying to make sense of what was real and what was not.

"We can still have something."

I looked into his eyes a moment, trying to read what he was saying, what he was offering or asking for. Was this guilt or truth or something in between? I had become an extension of Aris's self, and sometimes I think he didn't realize that I was a separate entity, not just something that lived both inside him and very far away.

Either way, it didn't matter. "Are we done here?" I asked, painfully aware that I had come to the taverna after him, met his gaze, led him into the alley. "I have to get back."

"That's it?" he said. He waited. I didn't move. Said nothing.

Finally, he shook his head and I watched him walk down the steps back into the garden of the taverna. Not his usual confident walk, loose limbed, with that absence of self-awareness. A heaviness. I sat back down in the bar. Nefeli gave me a look. Fady was gazing back over his shoulder. "Well," he said, turning to the table. "There goes the neighborhood."

"It's fine," I said to them both. I took a drink. But I had not prepared myself for seeing Aris in public, with her. I had not thought of how real it would feel, how final. Say what you will about it, our emotional dependence was significant. When we were apart we'd talk for hours on the phone, or online. He'd call me in the middle of the night to tell me something funny that had just happened. Other times for no reason at all. Maybe it was simply an intense friendship all along. We had all the components (affection, conversation, desire, closeness) but nothing to root it. I thought that was a question of timing, of logistics. But maybe it was not so complicated at all. Love is not an accumulation of traits.

I had never seen Aris look as sad as he had that early February morning when he brought me to the airport, after my parents' funeral in Athens. We had barely slept. I was convinced something was wrong, that he was sick, because when you lose something close to you, you expect everything and everyone is next. The plane ride was terrible. The plane rides are always terrible.

Now, as the musicians continued playing, as Dimitra sang, I lost track of the rounds of drinks brought over to our table, the little pitchers and the ice and the raki. At one point Nefeli put her hand on my wrist, as if to tell me to slow down. Behind her my mother danced a hawk-like *zeibekiko* in a yellow dress, but the lighting was dim and I was drunk, and when I looked around later I didn't see any woman in yellow.

On the walk home it began to rain, but I was so drunk I didn't care. Yet I hesitated a moment at the door when I reached my building. I understood then that part of my uneasiness those last two days had to do with staying in this place, not at Aris's. The assertive reclamation of this space as *mine*. Though I still hadn't been able to sell the home in Chicago. I hadn't been ready. Aris

had discouraged it, too, which I attributed simply to his Greekness; no one got rid of family property here. It was the only way
people seemed to survive. And to sell a family home is to reject
a history, to walk through a one-way door. Those first few days
in Athens, I had thought I'd fix up the apartment to get it ready
for renters. For some reason it hadn't sunk in that this is where
I'd now stay. Despite the pain of seeing Aris, the night had filled
me up: the music, the drinks, the dancing, and I felt that fervent,
liberating joy I felt nowhere else in the world.

I let myself in with my new key, turned on a few of the lights.
The apartment felt cozy and welcoming. I took a hot shower,
dried my hair, and drank a cup of mint tea, then fell asleep atop
the covers.

5

The Captain

When I woke the next morning I cleaned up the kitchen, the pan from the carbonara that we'd eaten in the middle of the night, and felt very sad. We had plans in Athens that evening with Eva and Aris and several others, but I wasn't looking forward to the outing. Usually Katerina and I went out closer to home in Kifissia; it felt a bit disorienting, going out in Athens with her, as if my two selves—the man who lived with his family in the northern suburbs and the man who lived in Athens—should not meet.

When we drove to the center for dinner, though, I felt calmed by all the lights, the traffic, the noise of the city. As I was admiring the violet sky, Katerina groaned. "God, Athens is so ugly," she said. "How do people stand it?"

I admit the transition from our cool leafy street to the grit of the center was a stark one, but I liked the traffic and the street art, and the rag-tag bunches of young people who hung out in clumps were as much a part of the fabric of the city as anything else. Athens, to me, is a glorious city; I have traveled the world and it's still one of my favorites. To call it ugly or a concrete block city, as Katerina often did, was missing both the point and its beauty. She didn't like New York City either, for instance. Katerina hated traffic, she hated chaos, and if she had her way she'd live in a quiet corner of an island, and that would be that. When in Greece she complained about it but couldn't stand to be away from it, she realized, which matched the sentiment of many of our friends: reject it before it rejects you. There was a brain drain: many had gone to Western Europe, Canada, the States, but unlike generations past it seemed no one was really happy with the decision, saw it as temporary. They were not making a new life but instead trying to keep the old one afloat.

When we parked the car and walked a few blocks down Kallidromiou—I knew the restaurant Eva had suggested was in the center but I had not expected to be back in this very neighborhood, where I took my long walks—I noticed she was tightly clutching her purse. Alone here I blended in just fine, I suppose, but Katerina in her blue silk blouse, her perfect eye makeup, her hair styled that afternoon—I braced myself for dirty looks. I wondered why he'd chosen this place until I realized Aris, striving politically, wanted to be seen out among this bunch: the people, the rebels, the intellectuals, the anarchists.

I hadn't seen Aris in years—this evening's plans had been arranged because his new fiancée, Eva, had long been a close friend of Katerina's—and even so I only vaguely remembered him. I did not yet know his history with Mira. He was younger than I, by nearly a decade, and when he stood next to me, I noticed that an outline of his body would have fit perfectly into mine. The same mold, scaled down by 7 percent. His shoulders were narrower, his hips thinner, and when I stood to greet him and we both settled into our chairs our eyes met, the eyes of the outsiders, the men brought in by marriage. I glanced at the others, all engaged in animated discussion; if anyone noticed my discomfort they didn't mention it.

We talked of insignificant summer things, he asked about our kids. Even though our obvious connection was politics, we steered clear of it, though he said nice things about my father, whom he admired very much. Our fathers, both well-known and revered, if not respected, had made their homes on the island. His father had already been in the public eye for his socially astute, acerbic novels, and when called upon he was still a powerful voice. "Few sons are the equals of their fathers," Athena says in *The Odyssey*.

I drank a lot of *tsipouro*. Everyone was talking about a reality television series, based off an American show, which was based off a Swedish show, where a group of good-looking strangers are dropped off on an island and made to compete for resources through strange games. I had not seen the show, but in this world, in this country, at this moment, it seemed in bad taste. But when I said so, Katerina rolled her eyes and everyone laughed. "Come on," another said. "At this moment it's *exactly* what we need."

A few people came by, snapped photos not so surreptitiously with their phones. Eva was regaining attention: fifteen years ago she had starred in a few Greek movies and some French ones, but in her thirties she had disappeared. Depression, near misses, and a string of bad love affairs had kept her in a constant state of neurotic attachment, unable to focus on her work. But with her recent comeback she'd become suddenly political, as if a new generation's Melina Mercouri. Her eyes, large and dark brown, had an unsettling depth to them, and she'd always looked at me as though she knew something I didn't. I had to admit that she and Aris seemed well-matched.

I think now that I was a little jealous, all that newness ahead of them. Katerina thought Eva was as beautiful as ever, but she often said this of her friends. Men never bothered with such statements. If a man was handsome we didn't have to tell all the women at the table about it. Or we didn't notice. Then again, if you grew up in Greece where men on talk shows slap women on the asses and adult women are called "girl" until they're fifty, perhaps you'd want to beat men to the punch, to take away some of the power by assuming it yourself. Later, Mira surprised me by saying that maybe being called a "girl" carried with it a certain air of independence. Before you became a woman, or a wife, the word was the same. Still, to talk so brazenly about other women in the company of women, there's something aggressive, demoralizing about all of it. Anyway. I have never quite fit with ideals of Greek masculinity.

Katerina seemed happy to be there, which gave me a certain feeling of contentment. But the conversation at the table, petty gossip disguised as politics, the chatter of my childhood, bored me, which had me looking around the taverna. It was then I spotted Mira. She headed across the garden, a confident walk like she'd been here many times before—that's when she saw me. Or, really, that's when I guess she saw Aris, the two of us together, and the look of confusion, even betrayal, on her face has stayed with me, particularly because then I had no idea what would have caused it, or perhaps because now I do. I had the urge to get up and follow her, say hello. To say I was going to a bank machine or to get cigarettes or even to disappear to the bathroom and out the back of the bar into the narrow alleyway. I even began to stand. All of this was happening undetected by the rest of our table, yet it seemed at that moment all eyes were on me, on us.

Aris's chair tipped back as he leapt up, but he caught it. His standing shut mine down, and it was he, not I, who walked after Mira.

At first I thought it was coincidence. After all, what are the chances? But coincidence is story, is it not? He was focused on her; he followed her. I looked around the table but everyone was engaged in conversation and no one noticed Aris slip away. Mira walked more quickly, in front of him. When she turned the corner, she looked back and our eyes met. I waved just as she was eclipsed by a group of waiters carrying trays in the air, another group of diners taking a seat. When they passed both she and Aris had vanished.

"See someone you know?" Katerina asked. She was smiling, in the middle of another conversation, looking around the taverna with curiosity.

"A friend of my father's," I lied, waving my hand in the direction of several tables.

Eva, on Katerina's other side, turned to us. "Where'd Aris go?" she asked.

Somehow I felt unaccountably guilty. I made an excuse for him: the cash machine, I thought, or out for cigarettes. Katerina looked at me oddly, and she and Eva turned back to the other conversation.

Where *did* they go, Aris and Mira?

I glanced around the taverna again. Later, when I thought of that evening, those minutes seemed to encompass the entire night. Mira's expression. My slow-motion wave. Their absence together.

A loud roar rose up from our table: the husband of one of Katerina's friends had told a joke. I laughed again. A laugh always disguises another emotion, whether it's pain or desire or shame.

An old girlfriend once told me that I only loved women who could not really hurt me. That my fear of commitment, my hesitation, was an adolescent longing for some perfect fantasy, a way of avoiding pain. I admitted she was right. Admitting and accepting share the same root, though I was having problems with the latter. Maybe I'm quick to try to find flaws in other relationships, to view them with suspicion, because I understand something was lacking in mine. But what. That is the thing. But what.

When Aris finally returned through the front entrance of the taverna, looking distraught, I felt a swell of retribution and rage—origin unclear—and relief. When Eva asked him where he'd gone, he tossed some cigarettes down on the table. I swear he looked at me when he did it, an aggressive smugness. I glanced around again. Mira was gone.

Have you seen those silvery, flying fish that glimmer over the water? It's only until they slip beneath the surface that you register what you've glimpsed, wonder whether the ship's wake sends them flying into air or if they're jumping, leaping on their own accord. You want to hold them in your hands, examine their wings.

*

The next afternoon at the airport, Ifigenia hugged me tightly and tied a few bracelets she had woven around my wrist. Nikos seemed unmoved. "See you, Dad," he said, in English. They had gone to an American school in Athens and continued in one in Brussels, and their American-accented English, so natural to my ear, still seemed strange coming from my children. Katerina hugged me tightly, and at that moment I did not want to let go. Though she had been more set on the separation, I know sometimes she wavered. I did too.

Perhaps this is why I drove back to our home in Kifissia. Yet I quickly found the silence disorienting, the absence of the kids, the television, Katerina's soft voice. I opened all the windows to hear the birds, the comings and goings of the quiet street. I didn't realize how noisy my neighborhood in Athens was until I experienced the quiet of the suburbs.

By midnight I was back on my street: Armatolon kai Klefton. I slipped out to the balcony and looked over the garden, lit up by the moon.

Minutes later Mira's door slid open. I wondered if she'd bring up the taverna, or Aris, or what I was doing there with him. I realized it was my turn to speak.

"*Kalispera*, Mira." I pictured her the way she looked at the taverna: a loose dress gathered around her waist with a string, hair loose, boots. When she walked away I could make out the lines of her figure, her ass. Her long hair was tied back in a ponytail and it swished back and forth like a flag.

"Hi," she said.

Asking her about Aris seemed aggressive, accusatory. I waited to see if she brought it up first, but she did not. Instead she talked about Nefeli, and her voice—low, a little scratchy—calmed me.

I was not thinking of sex, no. Not directly. But that night, trying to fall asleep, I was aware of her asleep on the other side of the wall.

*

My brother called the next day. He lives in Detroit, had followed me to Michigan when I returned for college, and never left. He studied economics, works in finance, and, to be honest I don't know what he does except that he does well. He votes Republican and is very punishing about the Greek situation. He thinks Greeks should pay back the debt, cent by cent, regardless of the suffering. He does not see it in terms of geopolitical complexity. He does not see it in terms of compassion. The money was borrowed; it needs to be repaid. End of story. Perhaps his own internalized shame.

Moments like this, I feel my anger rising.

To be honest I didn't think he was really calling for me but to inquire about our father, with whom his relationship was fraught, like mine. Our father's leftism, the junta, had frightened my brother, who came of age during that time. But his sharp turn to the right had been a shock to both my parents. My father could get over his living in the States—my mother, after all, was Greek American, from Detroit, and we'd lived there for several years when I was a child, during the junta—but this transgression was more unforgiveable than my brother's refusal to name his first-born son Nikos, after him.

My brother came to Greece rarely now. As a younger man he claimed he simply could not afford it, did not have the time, and now his absence was normal. He has always rebelled against my father while at the same time deeply needing his approval. Last year, my nephews, his two sons from his first marriage, showed up with their mother. She, my brother's ex-wife, recently remarried: another Greek husband, from Crete. This incenses my brother. My nephews say she's happy. She learned the language a long time ago, when she married my brother, and speaks it fluently with those flat, round vowels, the hard letter *ells*, the open, lax drawl. She's a kind, smart, sweet woman and I'm surprised she ever fell for my brother in the first place.

My brother had spoken to our father the previous week, he said. He'd mentioned elections, which at first my brother had taken as picking a fight, but it was clear he was not talking about recent or upcoming elections, not in Greece and not in the United States, and my brother had let it go. My father also mentioned helping Nefeli with a project, and my brother didn't know what he was talking about. Neither did I, I said. But what really worried my brother was that my father had asked about the twins, and when my brother said, No, the twins are Alexi's, he'd replied, Yes, of course. The babies.

They're not babies, *Baba*, my brother had said. The twins are nine, and my sons are in college.

Our father had laughed. Obviously, he'd said. I still think of them all as babies.

"Something felt off," my brother said. "Anyway."

"Yeah," I said. "And how *are* the boys?"

He exhaled loudly, a habit from his earlier smoking days, now a sign of distress. "They're well," he said. "Both have girlfriends."

I knew he meant this as some sort of marker of normalcy.

My brother often seemed irritated with his kids, which always baffled me. Last August, when they'd traveled to Crete with several friends, I invited them to come aboard the ship. They flew instead, but when we docked there I met them in Chania for lunch. I hadn't seen them in several years, and I was expecting arrogant young men with an American sense of superiority. But my nephews were laid back and very sincere. We drank beer together at the old port, sitting in fluffy white chairs, the two of them facing the water. They asked about the twins, about Katerina. They were concerned about the current situation, whether I had encountered smugglers or distressed refugees, whether I'd experienced anything firsthand while at sea. I thought of the dense network of shipping and warehouses, leather jackets from China, racks of cheap clothing that will end up on street markets in Skopje and Tirana and Plovdiv. Illegal stuff: heroin, hash, cocaine. Guns guns guns. Contraband and counterfeit cigarettes. And, of course, people: human traffickers moving bodies across the Aegean, across the Adriatic, into Italy and beyond. Or dropping them off on Crete's south shores and calling it Italy. I had only wanted to counteract some of that, inject some humanity into the inevitable process of migration.

But I'd lied and told them no, asked about their father.

They looked at me from over their large beer mugs. I could see my brother in them both—heavy brows, wide-set, nearly black eyes like our mother—but how my brother had produced such polite, open-minded boys was beyond me. One studied public policy at the University of Michigan, and, get this, minored in Modern Greek Studies. My brother had told me this on the

phone, going through the faculty lists and reading out their re-
search interests with scorn. *And our tax dollars pay for this shit*, he
said. I could not reconcile the brother I knew, with his disdain for
the uneducated, with this attitude. But me, I was impressed with
what my nephew was reading, what he knew of recent Greek history. And he was delighted, and slightly baffled, that I'd studied
with the same Shakespeare professor decades before. His Greek
was correct and elegant, with only a trace of an accent.

My other nephew was pre-med at Ohio State. When I asked
him what sort of doctor he'd like to be, he said he'd told his *father*
he'd like to be a surgeon. His brother laughed. They were at such
ease with each other, the biggest rift between them their college
rivalry, their kindness the most foreign thing about them. He
wants to be a personal trainer. That's what he told me. That my
brother would kill him if he knew. It's never enough for him, the
younger one said. And it never will be, his older brother said. Just
like your grandfather, I added, and they shrugged, a *what can you
do*. They took a selfie of the three of us and each sent it off to
their girlfriends. They invited me out the following night to meet
their friends, but I was leaving with the ship the next day. I paid
our bill, they thanked me several times, and I went back to work.

A few days later, I was asked by a commanding officer at the
shipping company, a man I'd known and liked for years, to leave
my post. I was being suspended. And I did not react well. I lost
my temper, grabbed his shirt before catching myself and letting
go. I had not acted out physically in a very long time, not since
I was in my twenties, those years after my mother's death when
even a brush of wind could send me into a rage. When I remember the startled fear on his face I'm filled with shame. He could

have pressed charges, called security, reported this, too, to the International Maritime Organization, but instead he calmly told me to gather my things and vacate my cabin. But my fury, shocking to him, was terrifying to me. Later, I called him to apologize for my anger. "It's a hard time for all of us," he said.

But there are protocols. My case, complicated as it is, is under review, and though I'm not ready to talk about it I'll say a few things. I may go into early retirement. Instead of following marine law I took things into my own hands. I suppose I wanted to be a hero. The company is sympathetic but I could have handled things differently, I know. This, the obligation of the office of the captain, hits all aspects of my life. I'm not saying I always honor my obligations. But they are there, and I always feel them. Maybe that's why I'm having so much trouble accepting Katerina's desire to split.

My brother knew none of this, and I probably won't ever tell him. It upsets me, talking of these things. One can only move forward, or try.

Despite his worry about our father, he was in good spirits. I asked him if he'd visit this summer and he grew quiet, said he didn't have the time, but he'd try to come soon. I knew he would not. While his first wife, the boys' mother, had fallen so in love with the place and the language, his second wife was less enthusiastic. Seeing Greece through her eyes has given my brother a renewed disdain for it. Their first and only visit was a disaster. She ordered iced tea at dinner, and when the tavernas did not have it she took it as a personal affront. She viewed everything in Athens as though it might be contaminated, was afraid to drink the water, to eat any fruit, to ride the train. She wiped down every surface with little wet cloths she kept in her purse. I wanted to tell him now that she could order any sort of iced tea, that there were organic juice bars and tea houses and vegan restaurants, but I knew that would not be enough.

"Go to the island, see if he's okay," my brother said. This surprised me. He had always exhibited such contempt for our father, but I suppose it was an inverse sort of guilt disguised as resentment. Me, I was the opposite, masking resentment with guilt.

I told him I was going soon for a christening, and we hung up.

Whereas my brother has always been on the offensive with our father, I am forever on the defense. What surprised me most was the disgust my father had expressed, when I was younger, regarding my decision to stay at sea. *You're escaping, you're running away*, and this to him was unacceptable. *Get a job closer to home. Get a job on land.* Our relationship had always been difficult—as a teenager I'd confronted him about his infidelities—so to see him take on the persona of a virtuous family man filled me with a mix of sadness and rage.

But the thing is, he *did* see himself as a family man, one who never abandoned his wife and children. Not for the love of another woman, not for a sense of independence. In this way he saw himself as loyal, as sacrificing other lives for the one he'd first chosen. To him it was the way of the world, the world of men, and he maintained both a fierce *no one will tell me what to do* attitude along with a deep sense of obligation.

Despite our differences, we share a nostalgia for the future—a dangerous, optimistic longing for what could be. It's what kept him in politics and what has kept me afloat.

6

Mira

Those first weeks I was in Athens, Nefeli, working hard for her opening, sometimes behaved the way she had that night out with Fady and Dimitra—unagitated, full of warmth. Other times, she acted strangely, as she had that day at the beach, speaking in non sequiturs or circles. Irascible. From time to time she was uncharacteristically quiet. Sometimes she stayed up all night in her studio, but it wasn't until after her show opened that I really began to worry.

But until the opening, when she wanted a break from working, I'd meet her at the new coffee shop several blocks from her studio, the one with the goat logo. I was calmed by the minimalist space, even its unapologetic trendiness, and when I walked in with Nefeli the baristas's faces lit up. I'd never seen her studio, which was in an old building that she and a few other artists used as a workspace. It was too private, she said, like offering a glimpse into the mechanisms of her mind. Only Fady had been there, but she made him promise not to utter a word about the project. Her reticence was born less of self-importance than it was of superstition.

But that morning, Nefeli had asked me to meet her at her studio. She had few things she wanted to bring and needed help carrying them. I'd woken late so I hurriedly dressed and stopped at my corner bakery for a coffee to drink on the way. It was one of my true Americanisms: walking through the city with a drink, which drove Nefeli crazy. I loved Athens in the morning: the way the early light hits the streets, the scent of butter and sugar from the bakeries, the crowded coffee shops with the lively chatter and the smell of smoke.

Nefeli's studio was not far from the small experimental theater on Mavromichalis, past the old movie house, past her favorite taverna, and fairly close to her apartment. Most of the homes were old beauties, some bright and well-kept and others in various stages of disrepair. One seemed like it had been burned in a fire, and the next was fit for a magazine photo shoot. Nefeli's building, though, was a large three-story gray corner structure I had walked by many times, noticing it mostly for the interesting street art that covered the walls: black-and-white Soviet-style drawings. On another wall was some stenciling: DEAR CAPITALISM, IT'S NOT YOU, IT'S ME. JUST KIDDING, IT'S YOU. IT'S OVER. The front door was huge, industrial, like you'd find at a loading dock, and I rang the bell twice. I wandered around the corner to see if there was another entrance; on the side of the building someone had spray painted, in Greek: NO HOPE. And below that, in English: FUCK MY DESIRE.

From the open window on the top floor I could hear music, and finally Nefeli came out to the small balcony and said she'd buzz me in. Her face was bright; creating something, to her, was the antidote to despair, and no matter what else was going on, when she was working, she glowed. There were two doors on the bottom floor: one was a dance studio, and the other door was unmarked. When I reached the third-floor landing, Nefeli was standing in front of her door. She wore baggy jeans and a white T-shirt with the sleeves cut off, her hair pulled back in a blue scarf.

"No peeking," she said, deliberately leaving the door open a crack so I could. She was in good spirits. The ceilings were high, and the space was huge. Behind her was a large table, scattered on it dozens of little blue scorpions, ceramic, with distorted limbs. I found them disconcerting. She slipped behind another dividing wall, which was where she was building the components of the installation, and emerged in a clean shirt, holding overflowing tote bags. She handed me one filled with school supplies and another of flip-flops in various sizes and colors.

The squat, as Nefeli and Fady and Dimitra referred to it, as well as those living there, was not far from the studio. It was an abandoned school turned into housing for recent arrivals, a cooperation between the refugees themselves, mostly from Afghanistan and Palestine, Syria and Iraq, and local anarchists and activists, depending on whom you asked. Nefeli was proud of the work being done there, and she wanted to show it to me. She thought it would be useful for my new project—one I admittedly had not yet started—on grassroots organizing from the eighties until now.

From the outside of the school, the tall cement walls, the steps going up, you'd imagine it to be filled with the voices of schoolchildren, which it was. Nefeli led me into the courtyard, where we were met by Nadine, an animated young woman dressed in various shades of mauve and plum, perfect eyebrows. That summer everyone's eyebrows seemed full and alive.

She clapped her hands together and smiled when she saw the bags of notebooks, the packets of blue Bic pens, the colored pencils, the markers for a dry-erase board. Nefeli quickly introduced us and took some of the materials and disappeared behind a door off the courtyard, where she ran a drawing class for teenagers and adults. In another room off the courtyard a meeting was in progress: men and women discussing, in English, the labor rights of immigrants and refugees, and a man stood in front of the room, interpreting. Later that night, Nadine said, the room would be used for a dance class. Through the window of another room I could see children from the ages of eight to twelve settling in to the desks: these were children who, most of them recent arrivals, had not yet been enrolled in Greek schools. The first lesson of the day, according to Nadine, would start soon: math. One girl sat on a bench, reading, while another behind her braided her hair. A third sat at the desk, vigorously erasing something in her notebook.

Nearby, some women sat on a blanket, holding toddlers. One younger woman painted the nails of another, and on a nearby bench an older woman read a novel, holding it at arm's length.

From across the courtyard a lanky older boy approached us. He held an infant no more than a year old, dressed in a pressed white oxford shirt, little blue shorts, and light-blue socks, his eyelashes like giant fans. In this new context it took me a moment to register that the older boy was Rami. He smiled, a big toothy grin, recognizing me from the other night. Because he was not in school, Dimitra had arranged various homeschool options for him. During his off hours he came here with Fady or Dimitra, helping with this and that; acting as a babysitter, even a translator for the younger kids, or disappearing into the corridors with the older boys, which made Fady nervous, but Dimitra insisted he'd be fine. Rami's spoken English was already excellent, and next week we'd start writing lessons together, per Dimitra's request.

The men at the squat were virtually absent, but the older boys, some nearly young men themselves, hung out in the back of the courtyard, away from the women and the children, and though Rami looked young for his age, at least to me, I could tell now that Rami was more one of them than he was of the kids who sprawled across blankets, drawing pictures and making crafts, writing with bright-colored chalk, waiting for their morning lessons to begin. Perhaps these kids were used to strangers dropping in as volunteers, and they eyed me shyly.

Rami watched, too, holding the baby facing out. He kicked his chubby legs and looked around the courtyard agreeably, as if taking in any new place, as if he'd just been dressed up one morning on his way to a family wedding and, by some glitch in time and space, ended up here. Which was about right. "Do you want him?" Rami asked, now extending him in front of me.

The little boy laughed when I took him in my arms, looking back toward Rami with a calm, taciturn expression. Rami put his hand on his hip, proud of himself. "He likes to see out," Rami explained.

"You're a natural," I told him, shifting the boy around. Rami said a few words to him in Arabic and he smiled, and then I began to whisper a little Greek rhyme in his ear and he remained transfixed. "I'm going to join my friends now," Rami politely said, "but maybe I'll see you soon?" I nodded and he disappeared with the others, all of them too old for that first class, I guessed.

The little boy stayed on my hip, happily looking around, but suddenly I felt ridiculous. What, exactly, was I doing there? Whose child was this? When I'd gone to places where I did not belong, as ethnographer, I allowed myself a certain sense of entitlement, however misguided or false it may have been. I allowed myself that sort of *deep hanging out* that my work entailed. But just as *myself*, as Nefeli's tagalong, I felt like an intruder. Then a young woman in chic dark jeans and a blue blouse, a blue paisley headscarf, hurried over to me and gently took the boy back in her arms, thanking me in Greek. Only then, seeing his mother' distress at temporarily losing track of him did he burst into tears. But soon he was giggling again, shrieking with joy. She kissed his nose, and along with two other women and a little girl wearing a pink backpack, disappeared out the front door, on their way somewhere else.

After Nadine opened the door of the classroom and called to the children, who stood to join her, the courtyard grew fairly quiet. I went to find Nefeli. I peered into her classroom but she was not there. I opened the door and saw the tote bags. A young man with dark, curly hair sat at a desk alone, writing in a small black notebook. "I'm sorry to disturb you," I said, in English, and asked where Nefeli was. He shrugged and said he didn't know.

It seemed wrong to walk down the corridors—families lived in classrooms. I walked to the front of the building to see if Nefeli was there and instead ran into Dimitra, who was rushing in to pick up Rami. She was surprised to see me and greeted me warm- ly. "But where is Nefeli?" she asked. "I tried to call her but she didn't pick up."

On the walk home, we stopped outside her studio and rang the bell. Another woman answered, her jeans covered in paint, and said she hadn't seen her. As we continued up the street, I turned back and spotted Nefeli on her studio's balcony, her hand up to her forehead, blocking the sun and watching us walk away. A few minutes later, she replied: *Sorry, M. Class actually tomorrow. Forgot you had come with me.*

Earlier, I'd asked her about her show: a huge undertaking, both new, never-before-seen installation work—which was what Fady was helping her with as a sound engineer—and a retro- spective of her paintings. The latter she described the way one would talk about shedding skin; though the foundation of her career had been in canvas, her new three-dimensional projects were what she was currently most engaged in. Yet she didn't see this transition as leaving one medium behind for another. This was the reason for the mixed show. What she wanted, she said, was to allow time to fold in on itself.

Rami walked ahead, wearing giant headphones, and I told this all to Dimitra. About her forgetting me at the squat, about the way she talked about her work. "It's like she's living in a slightly altered reality, one the rest of us enter and leave."

"How strange," Dimitra said, and sighed.

7

Mira

The weather grew warmer. There was a garbage strike. Bright-
colored trash bags filled the curbs and alleyways, and we stepped
over their overflowing contents and avoided the blocks that were
unnavigable. We talked about which stretches were particularly
foul—a stretch along Plateia Mavili, or the entire top end of Mo-
nastiraki. Athinas had become a sea of trash, and Omonia was
worse, so we avoided it completely. I was relieved my balcony
faced the courtyard and not the street. Still, we went out. There
was not much that could keep Athenians indoors.

My late-night conversations with the Captain continued, a
natural part of my evenings, a sort of self-narration for us both.
Our stories intertwined like a double helix. He spoke to me in
both English and Greek, as if he were still deciding which of his
selves to be with me, as if I were somehow defining that self.
Then, as though the vastness of the sea had swallowed him up,

he'd be silent for a few days, and then he'd continue a conversation I had all but forgotten. Getting to know him felt both wild and a little strange, and I became aware of him the way I'm aware of sun on my face: particularly noticeable when eclipsed by a cloud.

We stayed on our own balconies, but he'd sometimes pass a cigarette to me; one night we shared a few bottles of beer and another night, when I'd made stuffed tomatoes and peppers, I'd offered him one on a little plate. These were the only times I saw his face.

Those evening conversations felt like entering a confessional: the priest probably knew who sat behind the wall but in the public light of day would never acknowledge it as fact. And, as upon exiting a confessional, in the light I felt both unburdened and a little uncertain. Not that I had tumbled out of the dark of a confessional since I was thirteen years old, my last year in Catholic school, even though we were not Catholic.

Though I'd told him about my parents, the Captain asked me very little else about my past, about Aris, about the two serious relationships I'd had before him, and the string of less-serious ones in between, and I followed suit. Questions like that can come across as demanding. Instead, I told him my present: about Rami—his love of art and comics, his desire to be a writer, the way he'd asked, the other day, how you knew where to begin a story; the way I'd hugged him before I could attempt an answer. I told him about Dimitra and Fady, and Nefeli too, working on her exhibition.

One night, at the mention of Nefeli's name the Captain grew quiet. It was after eleven, and we spoke quietly. I knew she was close with his father, who he said appeared to be missing. He said this in a nonchalant way, as though his father often went missing. *Appeared to be missing.* I thought of the phrase. He'd spoken with his father's doctor and friends, he said. I asked if he was concerned and he said he'd go to the island soon. A friend's daughter's christening. He'd look in on him then. He'd grown used to his father disappearing over the years—spontaneous trips to Crete or Rome, though he never left southern Europe—and he was less worried about this silence than what the silence might imply. It wasn't the state of his absence, but the condition of it. The Captain said he'd notified the island police, but they had laughed and told him to relax.

Still, I could tell he was trying to remember the last time they'd spoken. When I asked Nefeli about the strange, confused comments I'd seen the Captain's father make on Nefeli's social media posts, she'd hinted at his beginning stages of dementia. I knew the Captain didn't see these posts because he was completely absent from the internet, never existed there at all. I hesitated. "I've met your father," I said, and I assumed he knew how.

This was not the first time I had felt a sort of barefaced intimacy between us when such an intimacy seemed impossible, an intimacy that was less comforting than it was destabilizing, as if time had jumbled and we existed both in that present moment and a much later, future one, with a shared history and the ability to understand each other without speaking.

"I feel like a beer," he said, suddenly. "Want one?"

I didn't tell him I'd already had two. For a moment I thought he was asking if I wanted to go out somewhere, but I wasn't sure, so I just said okay, thank you, and waited.

"I'll be right back," he said.

I stood to go inside and get some pistachios to share, and for a second I leaned over the divider to have a good look at his balcony. Two chairs, a small table, an ashtray, a large selection of plants, herbs. I recognized the oregano and thyme. From that angle I would have been able to see into his apartment except he hadn't turned on the light. When he appeared back in the doorway with two glasses he smiled to see me there.

"Hi," I said. I might as well have been watching him take a shower. That's how caught I felt.

But he didn't seem to mind. He handed me a glass of beer and I could feel him take in my entire body: face shoulders chest waist legs. From underneath his T-shirt I could see a glimpse of a tattoo under his sleeve. Nice biceps, nice shoulders. I reached over to touch his arm and thanked him for the beer. We each sat back down, hidden again from the other's gaze, and I felt desire, melancholy, embarrassment, joy.

"The tattoo I got years ago," he said.

I laughed. He'd seen me notice. Had I been staring? I took a sip from the small glass. Now what. I shifted in my chair.

"Only one?" I asked.

He told me it covered his left arm, onto his chest.

"Maybe you'll show me some time," I said.

He laughed. "Yeah?"

"This beer is great," I said.

"A pilsner, from Crete. Do you like it?" I could tell by his voice he was smiling, and I was glad he could no longer see me, the surely stupid grin on my face. I said, "Very much."

*

The front-door key I finally found in the wooden cigar box of keys and notes and coins my parents kept on the highest book-shelf, or maybe Haroula had kept it there. I also found some loose drachmas, and an envelope filled with three hundred euros, which was obviously my mother's, who hoarded cash all over the house. There was also an extra key to the island house, which I hadn't been to since before my parents' death—I would go soon, but somehow, leaving Athens made me feel anxious, as if I'd re-turn and this apartment, this balcony, the Captain, would all dis-appear.

Appear to be missing.

Aris had stopped calling, at least for the time being, and his silence was a relief; his absence easier to handle without his con-stantly picking at the scab. I had become used to the distance between us after all, and with that came a certain leveling of emo-tions—to be in a constant state of longing, of missing, was too much. When I came across his name in the newspaper, though, voicing support for the strikers or talking about the economy, I felt the hot shame of rejection renewed.

Meanwhile, I talked with Rami about story and graphic nov-els, which he said he was writing but was not yet ready to show me. He was barely a teenager but his seriousness of purpose was astounding. I spent a lot of time at the squat but often just ran er-rands: one afternoon, I took several kids from the squat to an eye check-up, and Rami had come along, wearing his own new glass-es and holding one of the little girl's hands. Two American college students who'd been working as volunteers, teaching English, had left abruptly—to them their volunteering was bundled up with vacationing, and the vacationing won—and Dimitra suggested I might fill in. So I showed up two afternoons a week. Afterward, I tutored Rami on his own: it was less like a language class and more like our own little book club. I loved his quick wit—so rare in a language that was one's second, third—a wit you'd think would belong to a much older boy. Then again, I often thought of Rami as younger than he was.

Some of my suggestions Rami rolled his eyes at: *those are for kids.* He wanted more substance: he was *writing a book too.* But Dimitra had suggested I keep it light. We read together, mostly in English, though he was learning the basics of Greek as well, the way kids just absorb language through their skin. English would be more useful to him, he said, because he was leaving. We'd finished *American Born Chinese* and *The Encyclopedia of Early Earth* and were beginning *Ms. Marvel* and *Anya's Ghost.* I'd ordered a slew of graphic novels online. I'd arrange them in front of him and he'd choose the next. He mentioned his brother in Germany often, whom he talked to on video chat; his family was growing anxious, frustrated at the slowness of the system, the failure of the reunification procedures. But he never directly mentioned leaving. Besides, the system all seemed so chaotic, so disordered, that nothing really seemed to matter. He'd left his home, alone, in the middle of a war. He'd made it here; he probably wasn't worrying too much about the legalities. But he seemed torn. "I love my brother," he said. "I miss him. But."

"But?" I asked.

He shrugged.

One afternoon after my class at the squat I waited for Rami, who was late, which was unlike him. I could feel my pulse quicken as I looked around inside. I asked Nadine, and Mira, who ran the classes for the smaller kids. No one had seen him. Dimitra didn't answer when I called, so I tried Fady.

He picked up and immediately apologized. "Sorry, lost track of time." Rami was with him. "Come by the workshop."

When I arrived, I heard Cretan lute music playing loudly and found the two of them, each seated on one of the ergonomic work stools. Fady was showing Rami how to use a leveler. "What's this?" I asked. Rami, in turn, demonstrated for me the way to use the tool, explaining what they were working on with an almost rehearsed bravura.

"He's a natural." Fady grinned, and Rami shyly shrugged.

This was of course better than idly roaming the city, or sitting in the crammed classroom at the squat with kids of all ages. Fady gave him attention, he spoke to him in Arabic and English and Greek, and he was learning something. "I wasn't much older when I started apprenticing," he said.

"I didn't say anything."

Later, though, I understood Fady had brought him to the workshop not simply to keep an eye on him but to create yet another connection, that Fady hoped Rami's interest in instrument making would somehow further tether him to their lives.

"I cleared this table," Fady said, his tone shifting now to business. "I have to leave for an hour or two, a shift at the asylum office. You can work here."

Whereas Leila would pout with any sudden change of plans, Rami was spontaneous, quick with transitions. From his small backpack he pulled out a Staedtler eraser, a few graphite pencils. He opened his sketchpad and, with some prodding from Fady, showed me several of his sketches of the workshop: Propped against a beige futon were two cellos in various stages—one brand new, not yet strung, and one in need of bridge repair.

I told him they were very good, and he smiled. But he became distracted by his phone, sending messages to his brother in Berlin. He looked up at me suddenly, as if he'd read something on his phone he wanted to tell me, and asked when I'd go back to the States. I told him I didn't know. This seemed to surprise him—it surprised me too, saying it out loud, since I had always left by the middle of August. When my parents had been alive I'd felt a heavy, unspoken obligation to live close to them: no more than a two-hour plane ride away. I had always been the parent, had always played the role they should have played with me. Perhaps it's why I'd never had the urge to have children. Not really, anyway.

Whereas the return to the States always felt like a natural, bittersweet part of my life, the cycle of the school year and the summer, the thought of going back to the States now felt flat-out depressing. It had never been easy, my departure signaling not only a return to the States and a goodbye to Aris and all my friends here, but also a return to the grind of classes, the endless emails, the university politics, an academic life obsessed with who worked the most, where productivity was not a quality but a virtue, and a passive-aggressive bullying that seemed to define my department's primary means of communication—a life I myself had worked so hard to obtain. The six years in graduate school, a postdoc, and finally a tenure-track job that always seemed like a dream, something that happened to other people. All the while my connection to Greece on a parallel and sometimes intersecting track: my dissertation-turned-book had been about women's experiences of the junta. Somehow, having Aris remain here in Athens, and the solid connection of my parents, comforted me. Now, the thought of being away from Greece felt unbearable, unfathomable, as if it could all slip away from me, and my life in the States felt as though it belonged to someone else. I watched Rami paging through his sketchbook. What would it be like, to not go back at all? To stay here, in Athens, or at least in Europe? There were universities, institutes, think tanks. Maybe I could find something.

More than ever, I felt deeply connected to the grit and beauty of Athens, coupled with the ghostly world of my memory and imagination. Say what you will about it—this country's structure of feeling was not one of isolation. America was a very lonely place.

Rami showed me a series of drawings, thumbnails. Most were of his neighborhood in Damascus, the first he'd mentioned it. Fady and Dimitra's large flat was much like his flat in Damascus, he said, the orange trees on the street, the smells, the balcony that wound around the entire building. I asked if *he* missed it, and he shrugged, said yes, he missed his friends, his classes and teachers, the particular place he liked to go after school for a snack. "It's part of your novel?" I asked.

"Maybe," he said, and smiled. I was worried this talk of home would have upset him, but I think equally upsetting was the idea that this life, too, was temporary. It pained me that his world, his emotional landscape, was so beyond my knowledge, and I was torn between feeling that I could only do so much for him, we could only do so much for him, and the nagging sensation that we could do everything, could do so much more.

I worked on my laptop and Rami read a graphic novel I'd brought him, ever so often interjecting to ask me the meaning of a word. I watched his face, waiting for him to continue our conversation, but he became immersed in his book, and we stayed in the sunny studio for the afternoon, until three, when Dimitra came for Rami, inviting me for lunch.

We walked back to their place, winding around bags of trash on the sidewalk. Dimitra told me about the students she tutored, a side job. Most of them went to the prep school where Aris had also gone: basically, she said, she wrote their college application essays. There was one student in particular, his parents ran a paper company or were big in shipping, she couldn't remember— "Does it matter?" she asked—who'd told her he'd only apply to Cornell and Berkeley as "back-ups," so sure he was he'd get into Princeton or Yale. "Well," Dimitra said.

We stopped in the pharmacy because both Leila and Rami had allergies. Rami tried to describe in English what it was that made him sneeze, and he switched to Arabic with Dimitra, who was not exactly fluent but could certainly get by, and at this moment I could feel two men glaring at us. I turned and caught one's eye—provocation, I know. But I wanted them to know I knew what sort of thugs they were, wanted them to see the disgust in my face.

When we exited the pharmacy, the two men—black T-shirts, black jeans, shaved heads—moved and stood in the middle of the sidewalk, already narrowed by a tree whose roots had dislodged several paving stones, which jutted out like teeth. Rami did not notice the men or their stares, or perhaps he did and had grown inured to them; he carefully stepped into the street to avoid them and self-consciously switched back to English.

Dimitra followed Rami off the sidewalk, stepping down from the curb. I refused. I held the eye of the larger man as I neared him, calling their bluff, waiting for them to part. But as I passed, one of them shoved me so hard with his shoulder that I lost my footing and stumbled on the broken cobbles, careening headfirst toward the tree. Attempting to catch myself, hands fumbling, I managed to avoid direct impact, but felt the rough bark of the tree against my cheek as I jerked and twisted my head away, inertia carrying me forward, sprawling me onto the pavement.

At first I was so stunned I could only stare at the ground. I tried to sit up, knees and hands still numb and tingling from the impact but already bleeding. "What the fuck," I shouted.

I drew my hand to my cheek—it felt as though I'd been punched in the face—and felt the ragged scrape from the bark of the tree. I was lucky I hadn't been knocked unconscious. My fingers came away with bright blood. I thought Rami was going to cry as Dimitra knelt down to help me up. The men watched, as if daring me. Then they turned and walked slowly away.

The pharmacist had heard me shout, heard Dimitra yell after the men, and she came out of the store. She began to assess my injuries, turning my hands over in hers, bending down to inspect my knees, brushing away some of the larger pieces of gravel.

I looked to Dimitra.

"You're crazy if you think the police will do anything," she said to me in English, as if reading my thoughts. "They're on *their* side."

The pharmacist brought us back inside and sat me down on a plastic chair. She carefully cleaned my hands and knees, using a pair of tweezers to pull out small bits of glass and gravel. Once she was done sterilizing the abrasions with Betadine, she applied the bandages. Then she brought out a small kit and began to clean my face. I smelled the sharp tang of rubbing alcohol moments before I felt its burn. The pharmacist was talking with Dimitra, telling her I needed stitches, as if I weren't there. I wondered if I should go the hospital, but the pharmacist seemed skillful, albeit a bit gruff. I winced as she numbed my cheek, prepared the needle. Rami cringed, unable to watch, and waited at the other end of the pharmacy, anxiously flipping through his drawings.

"You don't know what it's like here, in this neighborhood, with all the foreigners," the pharmacist said. I couldn't tell if she was offering this as an explanation or rebuke, whether she felt what had happened was an unfortunate accident or I'd brought this on myself.

I tried to turn my head, to protest, telling her how they'd tried to force us into the street.

The pharmacist didn't answer, told me to keep still.

"You're Greek?" she finally asked.

"What else would we be," Dimitra snapped. She instinctively put her arm around Rami, whose curiosity or discomfort had brought him back up to the front of the shop.

The pharmacist wouldn't look at the boy. "You should be helping other Greeks," she said. She had heard the Arabic, the English.

"Do you have children?" I asked.

"Three boys," the pharmacist said, rather proudly. I stared at her thick mascara. But then she realized why I was asking her this, finished off the stitches, and didn't say another word. I hate this way of relating, the way men empathize with rape victims because they have daughters. As if that's the only way. But shame can shut people up, and at that moment, I wanted to shut her up. I stared at her large dangly earrings, wanted to rip them out of her ears even as she sewed me up.

I walked home fuming. Dimitra had invited me back for lunch but didn't insist after I politely declined. Rami had closed himself off to us and I could tell Dimitra simply wanted to get him home. To retreat to their family.

I was fumbling for the key to my building when I heard a car door slam shut. There was Aris, stepping out of a new black car parked across the street. Somehow it'd been spared the red Saharan dust that had blanketed the city.

He called to me.

I turned to face him. He wore jeans and a gray T-shirt, hair wet and combed back. "Nice car," I said. I stood inside the foyer of the building while he stood outside, beneath the awning, the door open between us.

"My God, Mira. What in the world?"

I looked down at my bandaged hands and knees, raised my fingertips to my cheek, feigned nonchalance. "What are you doing here?"

"Alexi and I play basketball together." Rami and Fady also played basketball. Was everyone in the city playing basketball together? Why had I never noticed this before? This city's secret network. "We usually have a beer afterward. I was just leaving, about to go, but then I saw you."

I brought my hand between my eyes and squinted. It hurt my face. I wondered how long he'd actually been sitting in his car, but I was too rattled to be callous. "I'm going upstairs," I said. "I don't feel well."

He touched my cheek. I winced. I'd been given some pain pills but I had only taken half of one, and now I felt loopy and woozy and the pain all at once, as if the smaller dose had given me a random sampling of both pain and numbness.

He followed me inside and I was too exhausted to argue with him. We waited for the elevator. I did not want the Captain (Alexi? Had he never told me his name?) to hear Aris's voice, particularly after what happened between us the other night. Whatever that was.

Aris didn't mention that night at the taverna, the way he had accused me of wanting to pick a fight, cause trouble. All those years together we had never acknowledged a fight. Usually we just fell back into a rhythm. Things never got resolved but I don't really believe things ever get resolved. Dissolved maybe. Even as a child, when people would say something had a happy ending, I didn't understand. But now what? What happens after the book? The *after* was always the most interesting thing to me. Now what happens to the people in the book when I'm not reading about them? It was always perplexing.

Endings are false, anyway. Only beginnings ring true.

There of course was a problem. We never really fought, except those first few years we were together in Chicago. We had disagreements; sometimes we'd have misunderstandings. But we were always in a sort of visiting, vacation mode. We never had those difficult conversations.

It was not time to have the conversation we were about to have, but Aris and I had never been good with timing. I pushed the button for the elevator but then grew too impatient to wait for it. Aris was saying something as I turned to take the stairs. But I did not want to talk about our failed relationship now. I raised my hand to stop him from speaking. My cheek throbbed, and the three stitches felt massive, as if they traversed my entire face. I could feel bruises forming, thickening, underneath my skin.

At my apartment door, I could barely get that giant key into the lock. My hands were scraped and bandaged, and in my knee I felt a dull throb.

"Fucking help me, please," I said. My swearing in English in particular bothered him, though he swore in Greek all the time. I told him once it was a sign of intelligence but he'd only shrugged. Aris turned the key and we went inside.

"Who did this to you?" he demanded.

"Bar brawl. Soccer match."

"What match. Come on."

"Run-in with Nazi thugs."

"I can't tell if you're kidding."

"I'm fine."

I felt light-headed and walked out to the balcony, sat down at the little table. I wanted air. Aris didn't say anything. He placed his hand over mine. I had to fight back tears. It was all too much. I didn't pull my hand from under Aris's, but I didn't look at him either.

"Mira," he said. "I don't want to lose you. I never imagined it would happen this way," he said. At first he wondered himself if he were simply doing the right thing, he said, when Eva got pregnant. "I mean, I have feelings for her."

"Then why won't you just let *this* go?" I asked.

"Because you're my best friend," he said.

I told him he was crazy, pulled my hand away, and stood up.

He sighed, deeply. "This is not easy for me."

"Aris, I think I need to lie down."

I went inside, lay on the bed. He sat on a chair he'd brought in from the dining room, his head in his hands, as if for the first time aware of our boundaries. "Everything just happened so quickly," he said. "I had no one to talk to about it."

Because I was the one he talked to.

I stood up unsteadily from the bed, pushed past him into the bathroom, where I soaked a washcloth and held it against my bruised face. I could hear him outside the door. I leaned into the mirror and examined the black stitches on my cheek.

"Mira."

He opened the door and I watched him step behind me in the mirror. I turned to face him, propping myself up on the counter. He gently touched my knee, my cheek.

Something came over me then, something dark and devious.

He saw it in my face and I think it turned him on. I opened my legs slightly and he leaned in between them. He placed both hands on my thighs.

Yes, he was about to get married. I want you to know that I knew exactly what I was doing, and it was not an act of tenderness or a searching for some comfort. There was something almost violent about it. I wanted to claim some of him, to leave claw marks on his back and the blood from my cheek on his shirt. I wanted him to go back to wherever he was living now feeling dirty and disloyal, my scent lingering, as if I had my own grief to avenge.

And he wanted it too.

After, Aris walked out to the bedroom balcony—separate from the one off the living room near the Captain's—and lit a cigarette. I went back to the bathroom. I was convinced that if I turned my head I would see my mother standing beside the tangled bedsheets. I could just about feel her gaze on the back of my neck.

I had to get out of there, and I knew it would be the easiest way to get Aris out too. I had missed lunch at Dimitra and Fady's and was now starving. "I need to get something to eat," I told him.

"But I have to go," he said.

"It doesn't matter."

Outside, we stood beside his car. He gave me a long hug and a listless kiss on the cheek. As I walked away, his comment echoed from the night I'd seen him at the taverna: *We can still have something*. Of course I knew what he meant. I never thought that pureness between us, that freshness, what I thought was clean, easy love, could be altered. But I could certainly not *have something*, despite what had just happened between us.

Down the street was a new, trendy place that sold tiny little burgers out of an Airstream trailer housed inside an art gallery: lamb sliders with fig tapenade and goat cheese; beef with cheddar and bacon, Greek-style with mint and oregano, topped with feta. I sometimes stopped in for a drink, a plate of fries. The owner always smiled at me, small talk, insignificant flirting. Today I sat down, ordered a beer, and ate a plate of five. My mother's presence was palpable. I suddenly recalled her disdain when I'd come home one evening with a boyfriend and a little bag of hamburgers. It had been Lent, and my mother adhered to her Orthodox Lenten fasting, even though she had long before stopped going to church. Now, Easter had already come and gone, yet I could feel her disapproval so strongly that I worried if I turned around I'd see her there again, watching. Instead I licked my fingers, juice dripping down my chin afterward, like some satisfied, wild beast.

*

The next morning, I woke with a memory of the building's rooftop. I recalled it with such force and clarity that I didn't bother properly dressing before darting from the apartment, coffee cup in hand. I nearly locked myself out. The Captain was coming up the stairs after his run. If he thought it was strange to find me in pajamas, slippers, coffee sloshing on the floor, he didn't flinch.

He reached out as if he were going to touch my cheek, but he didn't, and we froze in that subjunctive, that what if, for a moment. I looked at his hand because I could not look him in the eyes. I wondered if he knew Aris had waited for me in the car, that he had come up. I wondered if he had heard him smoking on the balcony. If they talked of such things.

"I'm going to the roof," I said.

"I've never been up there," he said. "Not past the storage closets."

He followed me up the stairs, and for the first two flights we didn't say a word. In fact we both seemed to be holding our breaths.

On the last flight of stairs he stopped, and I turned to face him for a second. Even like this he was still taller than me. I caught a trace of grapefruit-rose and remembered something I had forgotten. The first time I met him, that first passing in the stairwell, I felt a flash of recognition that we might become lovers. Or a silent, mutual acknowledgment of some universe pulsing between us. It was a split second, like those movie theater ads that played a subliminal clip that had the audience racing to the concession stands for icy sodas and buttery popcorn. It's why new lovers glowed like neon—that harnessed energy.

"Aris asked me how well I knew you," he said. "Last night."

"What did you tell him?"

"I told him the truth."

The truth. I wondered what the truth of us was.

"He waited for me," I said.

"Yes, I know."

Though we had already been talking, though we'd had that little flirtatious interaction, it seemed our friendship truly began when we reached the landing, that moment we shoved open the door to the wash of sunlight. We stood in the middle of the roof together, and when I looked up at him I noticed him eyeing my cheek again.

Finally, he asked point-blank. "Did Aris do that to you?" His straightforwardness shocked me. I wanted to blame Aris for everything, but I laughed, so taken aback was I by the idea. I told him no. After I described what had happened at the pharmacist's, the Captain's voice grew thick, heavy. "It is sometimes too much."

I turned away from him. Someone had brought two small, red beach chairs up to the rooftop, facing Lykavittos. Positioned between them was a LavAzza coffee can, probably as an ashtray.

And there it all was.

Dancing with my mother on this rooftop. The closeness of her cheek against mine, the scorching sun. It is June. How young she is! We are dancing, and she is singing to me a song whose lyrics I only partially remember but whose melody runs through me so clear. I am five. I do not realize she is drunk. Downstairs large suitcases are flung open on the bed, clothes strewn everywhere, and my father is packing. We are leaving for the United States.

"I forgot about this rooftop," I said now to the Captain. In the sunlight his hair was not nearly black like mine or Aris's, but light enough that Greeks might call him blond. His eyes, without his glasses in this sunlight, the color of camouflage: brown and green and gray.

"To be honest I'd never thought to look," he said.

"Sorry again to have asked," he said of my cheek.

"It's okay," I said.

My father busts through the door, onto the roof. He is livid. Though prone to his own rages, he was a gentle man and had, to my knowledge, never hurt my mother. He rarely spanked me, and when he did he cried afterward. My mother and I are facing Lykavittos but we turn our faces back to him. My face looks suddenly stricken, as though I have just realized he is upset, but my mother has her head swung back, her hair spilling down her back, that golden-yellow dress with the embroidery on the sleeves. My father reaches out to take me from her and leaves my mother there on the roof, dancing.

A parapet was now built around the rooftop's perimeter, which I did not remember. I remember feeling worried she might fall off. *How much does she drink a day.*

I walked to the chairs but then passed them, to the ledge. The Captain didn't sit either. Nor did he talk. "I have a lot of memories here," I said. I turned to face him again.

My mother is on that roof with us, in that yellow dress; drunk, and singing. Another song we used to dance to: *I'll get myself a captain.* She's laughing, throwing her head back, and then she turns to me again and mouths: "He's married too, *koukla.*" She turns away and clinks the ice in her drink. Almost empty.

The Captain smelled of fresh sweat, of salt, of the tangy barb of his deodorant. He walked to the edge of the roof, peered over the parapet. He stood like a soccer player at ease: hand on cocked hip. Together we looked up to Lykavittos and down at the city, coming alive under the early morning sun. The Wednesday *laiki* was in full swing already, and the shouts of the vendors—cherries, apricots, lettuce—rose up in the air.

He knew I was interested in the histories of these Athens neighborhoods. He told me that when he was a child and would visit his uncle, who lived in the flat he occupies now, the neighborhood was much different. He pointed to the narrow road that rose up the hill and widened as it rose to Lykavittos: one neighbor had goats, he told me. And chickens who began their *koukourikou* before daybreak.

Very few apartment blocks lined this street then, he continued. "Before you were born, of course," he added. In fact, if you walked just a block or two down, he said, on the way to Mavili, it was like walking through a tiny village. "I can show you later, if you like," he said.

Sure, that would be nice, I thought I said. But I guess I didn't.

"Maybe you want to be alone up here?"

"No," I said, letting out a weak laugh. *Alone?* "Not alone. Thank you. I'm done." I turned to face the door but we were indeed now alone.

He pulled the door open, grinding it against the cement floor. I walked down the stairs ahead of him again, aware of him close behind me, aware of his eyes on my back. My shoulder blades tingled. At our doorways we greeted each other goodbye.

"You sure you're okay?" he asked.

I nodded. "Didn't sleep much last night."

*

Let me return now to that memory of my parents. Right before we moved, nearly thirty-five years ago. So I am five and my father finds my mother and me on the roof and whisks me away, leaving her there with her small green tumbler of something or other. My mother comes back into the kitchen fifteen minutes later, where I'm drawing at the table, a dismissive look on her face. I feel as though I've done something wrong, and I cry all evening. My father's silence penetrates the house. "She needs to be more careful," is all he says to me.

This is how I see it still. Like a film.

Or maybe it's that the truest, most defining moments were captured only in my mind, never film, never digital image. Now we capture everything, walk around with a self-awareness so acute that it becomes a lack of one. Look at me look at me look at me don't look at me.

You capture so much that nothing of your *self* will be left.

They say that children who are exposed to a language as babies always retain that language. That their brains will respond differently to it than non-native speakers, even if they are not able to understand or speak it as adults. I think of Leila and her ease with three languages, four, even, if you count the French she studies at school. But for her, Arabic and Greek will be forever imprinted, the way I suppose Greek is imprinted for me.

Maybe it's the same for places. I remembered very little about this apartment, and I wonder if what I do remember has come from pictures, or if what I remember has come from memories, but there are a few stark, vivid images that remain lodged in my mind. When I had shut the door behind me that morning, despite the earlier unpleasant memory, holding my coffee that had grown cold, I felt oddly impervious.

A few days after that incident on the roof—not with the Captain but the childhood incident with my parents—my grandmother scrubbed the hell out of the kitchen with Ajax. My parents were busy packing. I was in the courtyard with my grandfather, and I don't know why—maybe I had to use the bathroom or wanted something to eat—but we were coming back inside. Whatever the reason, I remember it was a sudden decision.

My mother was sprawled out on the staircase landing: blue dress, brown clogs, one of which had fallen from her foot and down a few more stairs. On the cool marble, my father held her head while my grandmother wiped her face with a towel. There was so much blood. And this: my mother was laughing.

My grandfather held me back. Stay here, he said.

It's amazing she broke no bones, the doctor said.

I remember my father relaying this to my grandmother. Only the big cut on her forehead, a smaller slash on her cheek. A scar that still remained. Stitches, a few tests, and that was it.

Why was she laughing, I asked. I did not know she was drunk. How could I.

Again. Why was she laughing.

Why.

To make your father know she was okay, my grandmother said to me. That's all. So we would know she was okay.

Is she okay?

She's okay, *loulouthi mou*. She's okay.

Just an accident, my little mouse, my mother said, home from the hospital. Mama's okay.

Like a rag doll, my father said.

It's the first moment of real terror I remember, and for years afterward I'd have nightmares of severed limbs, cuts, bodies bleeding, my father's fear-stricken face, the same one I saw last summer, when my mother was stung by a scorpion fish while swimming. *How much does she drink.* I would go into a panic and my father would count to five again while I inhaled and again when I exhaled, until I calmed down. He did it with my mother, too, her moments of such intense anxiety that she'd fling open our back door to take a deep gulp of air.

Our parents cement for us in midlife. Rarely in our minds are they the young adults who brought us into the world, or the vulnerable, aged adults who left us behind. They stay for us in middle age, which might explain why it's so hard to accept the fact we ourselves are middle aged. We have become the age of our parents, the pain of our youth crystallizing into something hard and physical. Bodily. But for all I know, I have created that dress, the vibrant yellow, its intricate red embroidery; I have created the blue one too.

But not the moment. The moment was real. And the music is even truer: I can remember two songs very clearly, both pop songs from the 70s or maybe 80s, the same artist, the lithe blonde my mother pointed out to me on the island many many years later, the one who'd briefly married Kazantzidis. She wore a spectacular green dress, and the crowd seemed to part as she walked through with her entourage.

That feeling of invulnerability disappeared quickly and I spent the rest of the day vaguely agitated. I did several loads of laundry, slightly calmed by the swishing of the washer, the quiet task of hanging up clothes to dry in the sun. Later, I called Nefeli to come over for dinner, but she didn't pick up.

8

The Captain

I had not been spying on Aris and Mira that day. I knew Aris had
been waiting for Mira, but I didn't realize he was still there. After
my shower, though, after making myself some pasta and salad, I
walked out to the front balcony, which got the evening sun, and
saw them saying goodbye in the street. They were not speaking,
only looking at each other. Then Mira turned and walked away.
She disappeared around the corner and Aris got into his car. He
sat in the car a long time after she had walked away, and the
whole image was one I wasn't able to shake. I had no right to be
either jealous or angry. If I had imagined anything between us I
had imagined either incorrectly, or inadvisably.

Aris was a good-enough guy, and I have always admired his
father. When I had asked Katerina if she knew who Aris had been
with before, she said Eva had left another man for Aris, and Aris,
as she understood it, had left someone as well. "But listen, he's

not like other politicians." I don't know what she based this on. I grew up around these men and this I know for sure: No politician is totally clean, and everything is a political act.

That night, I called my father's friend, Minas. Was he acting out of character? My father was a passionate man, and it's true he became a little unhinged from time to time. This was no secret.

"Getting old is terrible," Minas replied. Then he told me not to worry, that he thought my father might be spending time with Nefeli, who had a small cottage up in the hills, not far from his village. Nefeli often worked there, and my father kept some bees on her land.

I felt calmed by this, and thanked him. I told him I'd be coming to the island that weekend for a christening, my friend Dimos's first child, at fifty-two. I was relieved he didn't ask if Katerina and the kids were coming. They weren't.

"I'll see you then," Minas said.

I took a walk. A soccer match had just let out and I turned the other direction, toward Exarcheia. The other night on the balcony, Mira said men will never understand the experience of feeling threatened simply by the presence of men. She had walked by the soccer stadium on our street as a match was letting out, a losing one for the home team, and the testosterone, she said, had terrified her. She'd learned early on how to carry herself, how to deal with the masculine bravado that always felt a little bit dangerous. I already see it in Ifigenia, a way of holding herself. It frightens me. Katerina told me that a boy in her class had asked her to dance and she looked at him sharply and asked, "Why are you sweating."

Tonight, jazz and old rebetika came from the various cafés. An American couple walked ahead of me. The woman marveled at the nightlife; the man wondered if the area was safe. *What crisis?* he repeated, with performed perplexity. *What crisis.*

I wanted to grab him by his ill-fitting T-shirt; I had to clench my fists. What sort of person does not know that in times of crisis the bar business booms? I had to chime in. These people sit with the same two-euro coffee for hours, I told him. He responded that that was a bad business model. I gave up. His wife looked at me, as if hoping for more conversation, as if she might invite me to sit with them for a drink. All these Americans came here, wanting to know about the crisis, the refugees—from me, a real Greek!—and though I'm sure they were genuine, the idea of this disaster tourism really pissed me off. Years ago, this couple would have stayed in Plaka, and now here they were, in some overpriced, rented apartment, wandering to see for themselves whether it was safe, collecting tragedies and signs of blight as if this might make their trip more authentic. I remember Mira saying that people flocked to Athens because it felt edgy and only mildly dangerous, the safest dangerous place in the world.

I kept walking, passing three young cops on the corner. One looked into my eyes and nodded politely. I was too old to provoke authority, even when wearing a hood. I was no longer of the Molotov demographic, and with my lighter hair and eyes I was also not, to them, an immigrant. Another band of cops stood on the next corner. They recognized me and said "Good evening, Captain."

On the way home, on Mavromichalis, I stopped at a taverna my father had loved. An old haunt of the left. A small stroller was parked out front, and two bicycles. The guys working there had surely been born in the 1990s; they'd told me they considered themselves apolitical, which to me seemed very political. On a small shelf in the corner I noticed two of Aris's father's books and a few poetry anthologies. I looked at the display of photos on the back wall, near the bathroom. Sure enough, smack in the middle, was a black-and-white photo of my father and Aris's father, their arms around each other. I showed the waiters, who politely feigned interest. My young and laughing father soothed me a bit. I ordered some *keftedakia* and fries with my beer.

I was looking forward to seeing Dimos that weekend. He'd just arrived in Athens from New York, where he's lived for twenty years, though his parents still lived on the island, where we'd become friends. Dimos was a historian. We had all thought he'd go into politics, but he preferred to bury himself in archives and libraries and books.

The last time I'd seen him the twins had been three or four. I had been excited for his visit—the fog of having two small children made me crave adult company. Those days, I was rarely home for more than a few days at a time, so I suggested he stop by for a drink in the evening. I shopped for interesting new craft beers, set out pistachios and olives and graviera from the island.

This was a mistake. I don't know why I didn't suggest a nearby café. Somehow, I wanted him to see my full life, the chaos of children, the bustle of family. Maybe it was an act of aggression. I don't know. The twins had been in the other room, jumping from the couch to the floor, onto the cushions. Katerina was in the kitchen with Eva, who was fresh from a break-up, drinking wine and discussing the awfulness of men. Katerina's wistfulness for her pre-parent life showed only through her vicarious living through Eva's dramas, which she approached like projects for work.

But the chaos did not annoy me then; I remember feeling happy for a house alive. Fatherhood no longer felt so foreign. I heard Nikos shriek from the other room, and Ifigenia cry, and then both of them shrieking again. They were not shrieks of serious distress. I looked to Dimos to laugh—I had thought he might find it amusing, at least, if not charming—but he only looked uncomfortable. Irritated that we'd not have the sort of deep conversations we'd been having all our lives. He was adorable with the children, don't get me wrong, holding them up in the air, to their delight, but I knew then that our friendship would strain. Years earlier, when I'd invited him to the christening, he'd scoffed and couldn't believe I'd given in.

And now.

In those early years I had felt almost pleasure at the sight and sound of unruly children in restaurants, in airplanes, in enclosed spaces where the children weren't supposed to be unruly, even in Greece, where children were everywhere but adults still somewhat resembled adults. Adults behaving badly sometimes, but nevertheless. A relief, maybe, an admission to a club I had previously resisted joining, a closed society of new parents who looked over with compassion and pride and relief that the screaming child was not theirs, not this time. Sometimes in those earlier years I barely noticed it.

I'm not sure when the shift happened, but I've become intolerant to noise. Even children shouting with joy on a beach, or a mother calling out to her daughters, can drive me crazy. Ifigenia comes home and practices the violin and anger rises inside me, and Nikos with his loud scratchy voice, his belligerence, makes me lose my cool. Katerina's banging around in the kitchen makes me want to explode. At sea, even in moments of distress and chaos, there are always so many moments of deep, deep quiet, and I know Katerina could sometimes tell when at home I would rather have been elsewhere. Was it possible to love someone deeply and truly but not want to be in their presence? I don't mean *the kids are driving me crazy*. Something darker. How many duties as a father had I been spared simply for my comfort? Katerina knew that to keep me close she would have to do everything herself. And I suppose that was no longer worth it.

9

Mira

I wasn't planning on visiting Fady and Dimitra that evening—while in the States, sometimes weeks would pass without my seeing friends—but after Fady learned the story of what had happened at the pharmacy the day before, he said, "Either you come here or we come there."

When I arrived, I allowed him to delicately remove the bandage from my cheek so he could inspect the stitches, but Dimitra demanded we do so discretely in the entryway; she didn't want to upset the kids. Fady tipped my cheek up to the pale hall light, grudgingly praising the work. "There will be no scar," he said.

"Ha," I said. I hadn't told them I'd seen Aris again. But when Fady returned from the bathroom with a new bandage and a bit of antibiotic ointment, Dimitra had to reapply it because his hands were shaking. He told us he had a commission he needed to finish and disappeared to his workshop.

In the kitchen, Rami was doing Leila's math problems and Leila was, according to her, making slime. Some sort of internet thing, Rami told me, giving me his usual shy half hug. The two of them sat together, across from one another at the table. Leila had straightened her hair and it hung like a glossy curtain down her back, and with her caramel-colored eyes she looked disconcertingly like a young Nefeli. Rami concentrated the same way I used to, head cradled in hand, deep in thought. I used to fall asleep that way.

Rami paged through his old book, showing me drawings I hadn't yet seen, about a young boy in school in Damascus. Toward the back of the sketchbook he'd drawn some stark, pastoral landscapes, nearly dystopic, nary a human in sight. But I found it harder to engage him than normal, for whatever reason. Usually we had an easy rapport.

Something in the apartment felt strange, something that went beyond what had happened to me the previous day, something I sensed Fady and Dimitra were withholding. Finally, as if staying in the house would force her to address whatever it was I was feeling, Dimitra slipped her arm in mine and suggested we go out. She forced a smile. Fady was working, the children content.

We walked to a place on Strefi Hill—almost impossible to get a table for dinner but at that time of day, there were free places. It reminded me of Thanassis's taverna on the island: the multicolored pastel chairs, the stillness, the metal pitcher and small tumblers of water between us. The waiter, a bearded ponytail guy, a lovable anarchist, liked us, and the times I'd come in with Rami they'd spoken a mix of English and Greek. They talked about soccer, and I was surprised at the way Rami already had such strong opinions on the Greek teams and beyond. Our waiter was an Olympiacos fan, and Rami AEK, and when Rami made a joke about "gavros"—the little fish—I didn't even understand he was belittling the waiter's team, but the waiter laughed.

Dimitra and I ordered some baked chickpeas and some bread and split a small carafe of white wine. She asked me if I wanted to talk about Aris and I told her I didn't. We talked instead about Rami: his love for Leila and hers for him; the way Fady felt as though he had a son; the way Dimitra was overcome with the will to protect him, to raise him here in Athens, knowing of course his family waited more than two thousand kilometers away. "It would take twenty-four hours to drive there," she said. "I checked."

She told me he was curious that I had left Greece as a child and had now returned, and she wasn't sure if he understood— "No, he understands, I mean, accepts"—that the country he had loved and left would never be the same.

Dimitra reached over the table to touch my cheek. Discussions of politics, even in the home, made Rami nervous, she said, and she and Fady had begun to censor what they talked about, and when. He walked around with worry beads, like an old man, and told Dimitra he was a nihilist. "He knows what a nihilist is?" I asked. She shrugged and laughed. She showed me some pictures from the weekend. They'd gone to her parents' home, in Oropos. Leila and Rami were barefoot but in sweaters, facing the calm sea, the large island of Evia.

Rami's hands were both on his head, elbows out, and Leila's head, ever so slightly, was turned to him. In another photo, Rami's holding something in his hand and Leila is bent over to look, and in another they stretch their arms over their heads in a yoga sun salutation, performing for the camera.

It was the first time since Rami's arrival that he'd been in the sea, but Dimitra said he was okay, running through the sand and collecting tiny crabs. Then he and Leila sat at the large table on the balcony for hours, drawing while the adults talked. She said they were working on something together. Rami was an easygoing kid, usually difficult to rattle, and we wondered what experiences remained at the forefront of his imagination and what things he had buried deep. I asked if Rami had said anything else about what had happened the other day outside the pharmacy. Her brow furrowed, she tied her pretty curls back at the nape of her neck. We both knew Rami had seen far worse. The year anniversary of Rami's arrival would come in August, and Dimitra worried it would cause some resurgence of trauma, painful memories. We were all trying to keep those at bay, knowing of course that our attempts were in vain. Try as you might, you could not protect someone from grief.

The waiter brought a small bowl of olives, some fried feta with sesame seeds and honey. *Our treat,* he told us.

Dimitra smiled, thanked him, though she seemed distracted. Her jaw tensed. I thought it had to do with our discussion of Rami, whose impermanence deeply troubled her. Or maybe she wanted to tell me something else about Aris, though what else was there to tell. But I was wrong. "We have to talk about Nefeli," she said.

The other day, she and Nefeli had gone out to get some wine while Fady finished dinner, and she'd seen Nefeli slip a bottle opener into her pocket. A few days later, the two were shopping for Leila's birthday. This time it was pajamas from a shop in Syntagma, an American chain. Nefeli had wrapped a pair of pajama pants around her arm and pulled down her sleeve. When Dimitra relayed this to Fady, he told Dimitra that he'd gone to her apartment a few weeks earlier and the place had looked like a department store. He glimpsed a room full of clothing laid out on a bed. Her bathroom was filled with toilet paper and shampoo. Packages of T-shirts on the dining table. Makeup, pens. When he asked her what it was she was nonchalant, said it was for something she was working on, and walked him out.

Dimitra was now sure the flannel shirts Nefeli had given Leila for her birthday, the T-shirts for Rami, had all been stolen. She stopped eating, looked down at her food, rubbed her temples. "I don't know where to begin," she said.

I remembered that Nefeli had come by the squat with a bag of things recently—socks and flip-flops, notebooks and nail polish—that the girls went nuts for. Rami let one of the little girls paint his nails blue.

Dimitra sighed. "I did tell her we needed those things."

"Maybe she's just hoarding," I said. But we all knew that was unlikely. Nefeli hated to spend money. I wasn't sure if she was truly feeling destitute or if her theft was some sort of political act.

"I'm not sure what we're supposed to do," Dimitra said, popping an olive into her mouth.

Added to the litany of issues we were dealing with that year—strikes, neo-Nazis, the various facets of the vague, all-encompassing "crisis"—Nefeli's petty shoplifting seemed low on the list. But something about this news unsettled me, as it had clearly unsettled Dimitra. I thought of Nefeli's strange outbursts the day we'd gone to the beach, her recent combativeness each time we'd met for coffee. I knew when she was planning a show she'd often go through manic phases, and once she'd finished, she'd slip into a depression until the artistic well began to fill again. A familiar pattern to be sure.

Fady showed up as we were leaving, and the three of us walked. We stopped at a square, lively in the evening, with children running around and adults on benches, having drinks in the cafés, walking with friends. "The sounds in the *plateia*," he said, "the shouts of mothers, the squeals of children, the music of the voices. I've been recording them everywhere. You go to Berlin, to Paris, to Dublin, to New York: the voices don't sound this way. But in Gaza, in Cairo, in Aleppo: from afar, I would not be able to tell the difference. Sofia, Thessaloniki, Istanbul: these cities are Balkan. But Athens belongs to the Levant."

As always, I marveled at the changing light: it is orange, it is gold, it is lavender, it is dusk. Just before the sun disappeared, we stopped in a shop selling leather backpacks, like tourists, then a bouzouki/lute shop whose owner Fady knew, and an eclectic used bookstore with lots of foreign books. We walked through a dark residential area: the neighborhood had been working class but recently artists and young people and their fancy European strollers had moved in, and in the distance we heard music, saw lights. Another thing I loved about Athens: the way you could move through it on foot, from neighborhood to neighborhood, the night unfolding as you walked.

On the corner was a bar that seemed to glow red, rose, violet. The bar was crowded with people vying to order a drink, but we sat at a tiny table in the corner of the back room, looking out at the bar, the street. To our right was a large window, open into the night. Dimitra and I had Campari and soda, and Fady ordered some variation of a Negroni. Our ice cubes were shaped in the Greek alphabet.

An eclectic place, self-aware: a small vintage refrigerator was mounted above our heads, an old red bicycle, a transistor radio. Two Italian men next to us—clearly so by their body language—charmed two Greek Australian women. They spoke in English, broken but alive.

Fady eyed them with both envy and marvel. "Here, they'll also always be expats," he said. "If you're from Afghanistan, Iraq—even Bulgaria, Albania. It doesn't matter: foreign national at best. Migrant. Refugee. *Sans-papiers.*"

I wasn't sure if he was talking about himself, or Rami.

"You don't know how easy you have it," he said. "The options."

I didn't know what to say. His voice was not blistering, nor was he wrong. "You didn't come here as a refugee," I said.

"Not here, no. But I was, as a child. You're aware of the fragility of everything, always. That at any moment it might all implode."

"And in Germany, for Rami?"

He was quiet, as if I hadn't spoken, and deep in thought. "But I *am* a refugee," he said finally. "I'm not ashamed of it. Why should I be? I'm also a violin maker. And an artist. And a father. Husband. Exile. Many things."

Dimitra put her hand on his. He shrugged. "Maybe in Germany it will be different," he said.

I worried. In Germany it might be worse.

10

The Captain

Though I was staying in my father's house, I still hadn't seen him.
When I'd arrived, I'd found the bed was made; the place looked
clean. His dishes—an espresso cup, a saucer, a spoon, some plates
and forks and knives—remained in the dish rack. It would not be
unlike my father to suddenly meet a woman and disappear. As he
got older, though, and as he felt his own relevance slipping away,
his disappearances worried me.

I checked the closets for his two small suitcases, hard, light-
blue Samsonites that he'd had since the 1970s. Both were there,
but his small blue duffel was not. Strangely, I felt some relief
seeing them, hoping he was indeed in the hills with Nefeli as the
novelist had thought. He did not attend the christening.

Aris did, though, and he invited me for a drink the next day.
We agreed to meet at the port, at the café associated with the
distillery near our fathers' village.

There was not much wind now, and the day was warm. I ordered a beer and drank it quickly, eating the pistachios the waitress placed before me. When she brought my second round, she was distracted by someone who had entered. I turned to see what had brightened her so, and there stood Aris. He greeted her politely and then spotted me, moving across the café to join me at the table.

He'd barely had a chance to sit when the waitress reappeared, beaming at Aris, who flirted back with her. He ordered an ouzo, glanced at my beer, and changed his mind. "And would you bring us some more nuts, please." The waitress seemed happy to fill his request, and had he kindly asked her to unbutton her shirt she would have. He was the type of man who eyed women with that particular aggressive blend of admiration and possession.

I don't know why I was so angry.

We sat on adjacent sides of the table, so I had a view of the harbor and he had a view of promenade. Eventually the evening volta would begin. Right now the only people out were the tourists whose skin was least suited to the sun.

We exchanged pleasantries about the christening, about when we'd last been to the island.

"We met when I was a child, you know," Aris said. "You were visiting for the summer, from university. I remember your Michigan T-shirt: a bright orange with blue letters. When we got home that night I asked my father for a shirt like that."

This admission startled me. As a young man, I'd admired his father; had even imagined being a writer myself. Now here was Aris with political ambitions. We'd been born to the wrong fathers. Or perhaps there was no difference.

The waitress arrived, gently placing each item on the table, first Aris's beer, then the frosted glass, then the small dishes of peanuts and olives. He smiled, offered her his studied attention in exchange, as if they had rehearsed their roles in this transaction.

"Katerina didn't come," he said.

"Still in Brussels," I said. "They'll come for the summer, when the kids finish school."

Aris poured his beer into his glass. His mentioning of Katerina felt deliberate and loaded. But I was still thinking of the T-shirt. It was more yellow than orange, Michigan's maize and blue. I had saved it for years. It was probably here, in my father's house. I remembered that particular summer, the T-shirt, but not Aris the boy.

It was disconcerting to think of him as a child and me as a fully formed adult, the age where children were not even on my radar but I, an older college student, was on his. Did he see his own age in my face? To see us sitting together you wouldn't think we were a decade apart. I don't think so anyway, but we never think we look as old as we do; age is something imposed on us. Our inner lives remain the same. Or do they?

"Do you see her often?" Aris asked.

"She and the kids return for holidays, long weekends. Sometimes I go there."

"I meant Mira," he said.

I didn't say anything. I thought of her reach for my arm, grazing her fingers over the exposed ink.

"She hates me," he added. "Maybe she should."

"She hasn't mentioned you." A punishing line, and with a bit of pleasure I watched it register on his face. What did he want with Mira? He seemed unable to let her go even though he was the one who'd left her. I'd noticed some Mira-isms in his speech, and they irritated me. Things I had picked up too: inserting an English all-purpose "like" into a Greek sentence: "*kai eimai* like." I don't know if he was looking for absolution or information, but sitting near those sailboats, I felt as if I were somehow betraying Mira. I have always thought loyalty a strange thing. We think it has to do with history, with oath, but it is nothing of the sort. It's an impulse.

Aris then began to recount highlights of my father's career, as if he were auditioning for the old man through me, or fishing for something I couldn't see. The truth was that my father's politics both did and did not concern me. He was always hoping to reenter politics, to find a moment that might make him feel whole again, but now with his deteriorating mind I'm sure he understood he could not. A warrior without a war. I did not share this with Aris.

The previous time I'd visited my father here on the island, I'd found on his shelves a memoir by the poet Manolis Anagnostakis, who'd written that the most exciting time of his life was when he was constantly being followed, that any minute he could be arrested and sent away. It gave him meaning. My father had prided himself on being a rebellious, revolutionary voice, yet now no one listened to him at all, let alone saw him as an icon. I had not asked what he thought of the young generation of politicians, but I can imagine: *Babies,* he'd say, *doing their yoga, changing diapers, going to the supermarket.* Referring to the men, of course. To him, the women in politics were invisible.

Whether his politics concerned me was irrelevant; I was always in its path. When I was younger he and a group of his allies were involved in some scandal, and that's when I made my first escape. As far as I could get from Greece without going to the moon. To be off-land, on the other side of the planet, no ground connecting us. To stay at sea somehow, stateless. Rootlessness was my anchor.

"Any advice?" Aris said finally. I knew from his smile and the tone of his voice that he was no longer talking about my father, or politics, that he'd returned to the topic of Mira. Or maybe we'd been talking politics this entire time. "As the son of a politician, that is."

"Not much different than being the son of a novelist," I said. "Laundry hanging on the line." Because my father had been almost a compulsive philanderer, or perhaps despite it, I did not chase women. Or maybe I did. I'm not sure. But with Aris there, I'm ashamed to admit I didn't care if he thought I was exactly like my father.

Aris looked at me over his tall beer glass, leaned in a bit. "She's still important to me."

Was this a confession, a defense, or a threat? I said nothing.

Then the waitress returned and they resumed their outrageous flirting, and when she left the table Aris looked ready to continue our conversation but Eva had appeared, walking toward us in a flowered dress, her hair shiny and clean, well-rested and eager to be with her fiancé again.

I invited her to join us, but Aris stood and said they had plans. We fought over the bill enough to play our roles, but I insisted, kept my hand covering it on the table, and Aris was eventually forced to concede.

After they left, I waved to the waitress, who had disappeared, a bit pouty after Eva's appearance. I asked for another beer and stared out at the sailboats, the slow, metronomic swaying of their masts.

What I also remember from that summer: I was back from college, and one particular night I came out of a bar near the port and saw my father's friend Minas with a much younger woman. She was sitting on one of the low walls at the edge of the sea, and he was standing in front of her, running a hand up and down her leg. Braided brown hair, cut-off shorts, a bright-yellow embroidered blouse, turquoise bracelets on her wrists. I was twenty-one, and she was not much older. The jeans were cut so short that the pockets hung out below the hem.

Minas, then with a full head of shiny black hair, held one of those dangling pockets between his thumb and forefinger while the rest of his hand moved underneath. There weren't many people around, but even had there been they were behaving as if they were completely alone. She playfully moved his hand away, but I could tell that he had put his hand there many times before, made her throw her head back in pleasure. At the time I felt disgusted by him, as I knew and liked his wife, but I thought of that young woman for weeks after that, when I was alone with myself: her heavy eyebrows, her full lips, the long muscles of her legs. A few years later, when Aris's father had written about two couples and a love affair, Minas had refused to speak to him for over a year, claiming he'd taken details of his life. Minas had thought he and his lover were hiding in plain sight. In reality, they were just in plain sight. Years later, I'd asked Minas about it. Everyone knows everything, Minas had said. But what had really surprised him was that Aris's father had sworn he had not been writing about him. He was, in fact, writing about himself.

I had told Mira about this. She had read the novel. "It's always the jilted spouse who feels like a fool, but everyone knows they're the least foolish of the bunch," she said. Then she was quiet, and I heard her shift in her chair. "I guess the novel absorbs everything around it. But the things we think we see in novels," she said, "are the ways we want to see ourselves. Besides, are our lives really that original?"

What is in store for any of us besides the sins of our fathers? Sins we run from until we commit them ourselves? Though my father was absolved of any wrongdoing after his political scandal, the shame remains, the shadow around his name. Who stayed loyal to him has shaped his life. I always have acted as though his life was of no consequence to me, but of course it has been what has most shaped me. It was how I was formed. It doesn't matter that I drifted so far away: he was, he is, like a city hanging on a high cliff, impossible to ignore.

I was tired of all these men behaving as if there were no consequences. I suppose I had been one of them myself.

When I arrived back at the house, sleepy after all the beer, my father was still nowhere to be found. I lay on the bed, flat on my back, replaying the conversation with Aris to myself. I thought of the T-shirt he'd mentioned and jumped up to paw through the old chest of drawers. I kept some clothes here, mostly old things to sleep in or wear to the beach.

Sure enough, there was the shirt. I tried it on. My tattoo, which I didn't have then, peeked out of my left sleeve, the tentacles of an octopus. I had been skinnier. How much of that young man, before college, before the navy, before children, was still left in me, and what had the child-Aris seen? Did he still see the cocky twenty-year-old kicking a ball around on the beach?

I placed the T-shirt atop the dresser. I intentionally buried old shirts in my drawers so Katerina would not notice and therefore not throw them away. Now I suppose I wouldn't have to worry about that. All these last moments; my days had become populated by them.

The final months of my time on the Pacific, before I was to marry, I was nearly crippled by last moments. Midwalk through a bustling market in Ho Chi Minh City, I'd think about how I'd never walk through here again, never smell these stalls with those stinky, delicious fruits; these places where I bought fabric for finely tailored shirts that I still own, spending what there would be half a monthly salary. I'd never hear the particular cadence of the language, never sip that strong coffee. I'd probably never again feel the quiet stillness of Kyoto, where no one even used a horn; or pull into the spectacular port of Shanghai. The tenderness of those places for the last time, as touristy as my gaze was, was so crippling that in some ports I could barely leave my cabin. My crew would leave for dinner and I would tell them I did not feel well, that I needed to catch up on work. I fell in love in Casablanca only because, as I realize now, I knew it was a last moment, a traveler from London whose father was Irish and mother was Egyptian. Nothing happened between us, nothing physical, that is, but I even thought about her during my wedding, and when the doctor who delivered the twins had the same corkscrew curls and perfect eyebrows, I could feel it in my groin, the twisting throb of closing opportunities. I felt it again today, like descending deep into the bowels of the ship, the recesses of the engine room, the heavy doors locking shut behind me. Lights out.

*

I dreamt of Aris and Mira, but only Aris's face was clear. Mira was like a character in a book that I felt I had both vividly imagined yet could not entirely see—long hair, a shoulder, her wrist stacked with bracelets. I was conflating that drink with Aris and that time I saw her in the taverna in Exarcheia. I was imagining her walking by and seeing us there. In my mind I saw Aris get up and chase her through the crowd. I saw his petulance and her anger, then his anger and her petulance. Her lips dry from the heat, her eyes accusatory; the way her cheek still held a faint pink mark. He touched her hair and then her hip and guided her off the path of the street, next to a postcard stand and a kiosk, where she bought bottle of water, took a long drink, and wiped her chin and throat with the back of her hand. There was something wild about her, unpredictable. She made no eye contact while he talked. The way he touched her hair before they parted, the way it felt salty and textured, the way her back moved away from him into the crowd.

Of course I hadn't seen *any* of this. I had simply imagined it to be true. I'd only seen them interact twice. First, that night at the taverna, when they quickly disappeared behind the grape trellises, into the alley. And again while I watched from my Athens balcony. Yet I remembered these things as if I were recalling his memory. As if I were he. As if I were there.

I quietly went out to my father's balcony and looked over the valley, lit up by the moon.

11

Mira

Nefeli did not attend her own opening. She did not acknowledge the flowers we sent the morning of, nor did she respond to any of our messages, as though the show she'd worked so hard to complete was not happening at all.

When I arrived at the museum, people were clustered outside—talking, smoking. I found Fady and Dimitra and the kids. Leila had dressed the part of a young artist herself, with her dark glasses, her black clothing. Rami wore pressed jeans and a pressed paisley shirt, a blue sport coat, his hair all messed up with product (Leila, no doubt), and new heavy-framed glasses just like Fady's.

"Hey, handsome," I said, and Rami grinned his toothy grin. I took a picture of Fady and Rami, their arms around each other, now looking very seriously at the camera.

On the side of the museum, WELCOME was painted in a dozen languages, which was not part of Nefeli's installation but provided an interesting juxtaposition—all that earnestness. But her installation comprised a dozen bright-red megaphones, each the height of an old phone booth or a kiosk, which lined the sidewalk in front of the building and then the road. I wasn't sure what they were constructed of—wooden frames with painted, papier-mâché exteriors, I guessed. They each held a camera to film street activity, projecting the images to a room filled with screens in the gallery. A few other megaphones were installed across the city: near the university, in a square in Petralona, and outside the Victoria train station. These contemporary street images were being juxtaposed with footage of historical news footage. It was a project about surveillance and protest, and also the distortion of time and sound—the manipulation of sound through time. And, as Fady added, the silence of the current moment. The megaphones, whose bells faced the sidewalk, captured images rather than projecting sound.

Wandering along the line of megaphones, weaving between the guests with their cocktails, I wondered who was watching us inside. What moment in history this moment of mine was superimposed upon. Somewhere within the museum I wandered through time.

The gallery inside was crowded as well, and despite Nefeli's absence, the mood celebratory. We kept watching the door for Nefeli. Leila and Rami drifted ahead of us as Fady and Dimitri reintroduced me to several of their friends. As I watched Rami walk away, I noticed the worry beads in his back pocket.

Eventually I drifted away from the conversation myself. In the corner of one of the rooms stood a gaggle of young artists who were in love with Nefeli; the church paintings on the island where she was exiled as a student during the junta had recently gained a small cultlike status. One was a self-portrait that Leila stood in front of, studying. "You can't do a self-portrait until you're fifty," Nefeli had always told me, though she admitted to many in her early career. Acts of self-involvement, she said, rather than self-assertion. Here, the eyebrows on Nefeli's face were blue, and when you looked closely you could see they were actually scorpions.

In another room were the soundscapes Fady had worked on with Nefeli, which activated when you walked through the seemingly empty room, though in some places the sounds were distinct and in others they were overlaid—something about cones of sound. I found Rami here, wandering slowly back and forth, and together we listened to the sounds of laughter and children playing and the tinny calls of the *paliatzís*, the shouts of men in the *laiki*. High heels tapping on marble, the screech and rumble of the metro. Chants of protesters and chants of the liturgy.

After an hour or so, Fady and Dimitra said they were ready to leave—the kids had homework—but I lingered. I suppose I had begun to feel an anxiety about Nefeli's absence, still hoping she'd make a late appearance, knowing deep down, of course, that she wouldn't. I walked back through the gallery a few times, particularly taken with the soundscapes. I asked around, but still no one had seen her. I knew deep down that her absence was part of the show itself.

I was in the largest gallery room, with the megaphone projection screens, when Dimitra, Fady, and the kids walked past the installation outside, Rami looking down at his shoes, smiling, listening to Leila talk with her hands. Then, they all stopped to look at something not in the frame. I felt a pang of nostalgia for something I couldn't name. A sense of something missing.

On the screen I watched Dimitra talk in animated silence while Fady and Leila and Rami listened intently, their faces tilted sideways at the same exact angle. What was interesting about this footage was that the backgrounds kept changing; you might see the same images but never in the same order. Fady said Nefeli had programmed the footage film loops to continue to splice in new ones. Now the screen backdrop was the Polytechnic tanks. When they disappeared from view, the backdrop changed to a scene of South African apartheid. Then footage of hundreds of Bosnian refugees walking a dirt road.

Then suddenly there was Nefeli. Standing close to one of the cameras so it captured her alone. But I realized that I had no idea *when* this had taken place, because I'd been startled to see myself just a few moments ago. One minute I'd been watching Fady, Dimitri, and the kids depart, and then suddenly there I was arriving with them. Because the footage from this evening on the sidewalk was being added to the historical footage, looped in in random fragments as it accumulated, it was hard to tell at any given moment whether you were, in fact, watching a feed of something outside that had taken place an hour ago, ten minutes ago. So this could have been an image of Nefeli from earlier this evening, or weeks ago as she tested the installation. It could have been right now.

I had done a decent job not thinking too much about all these absences, those both prevailing and impending, but in the silence of the video installation, in front of that large screen, I *felt* them. We have our wounds and our desires and they wind around us like unraveling metal sculpture, like barbed wire.

On my way home I walked by her studio. Faint music streamed from her window. The street was dark, except the glow from her studio, as if the only things that mattered were the things inside that large, high-ceilinged space, those old walls, Nefeli still hard at work, racing against time.

PART TWO

12

Mira

June arrived in Greece like the return of a loyal but evasive lover. The early May cold snap I'd been greeted with was now balanced by an early heat wave. But we were invigorated by the warmth before its blankness exhausted us. Sundays we swam, staying at the beach until the sun disappeared, and when we came home we'd sit on someone's balcony, wanting to extend the day. Temperatures soared. We counted swims. I thought of inviting the Captain to come with us, but I didn't. He'd be leaving soon again, but I didn't ask him exactly when.

Athens felt familiar and foreign and hot. The mood was sometimes defiant and sometimes bleak. Refugees continued to arrive on the shores at an alarming rate, so frequently that it unfortunately normalized, became a part of the Greek reality, whereas coverage of it seemed to have disappeared everywhere else. The circus of US politics dominated foreign headlines, Greek ones too. Greeks, meanwhile, remained overwhelmed, and the international media did not know what to say. People posted news stories with a sort of perfunctory numbness. There was a spate of suicides: a woman shooting herself in a public square, another couple jumping from a balcony. I met with an old friend who'd lost her job; she'd moved back in with her parents, near Patras. At least we have the sea, she said, knowing damn well it was not enough. Another friend sold his family apartment to a German couple, who'd rent it out on Airbnb, adding that Airbnb would destroy Athens just as it had Barcelona. He was unwilling to discuss it with me any further. Dimitra's sister moved in with her best friend, and they taught yoga classes in their living room. It's the new order of things, was all she said.

Since her show had opened, Nefeli had grown particularly agitated, constantly wanting to adjust things, showing up at the museum in the middle of the night, asking the guards to let her in, calling the curator to shift things around, calling Fady to edit the sound, constantly splicing new things into the video. Nefeli was in a constant state of revision. It was as if her show were a living, growing, breathing thing. This, of course, made it all the more interesting, with people stopping in every few days to see what had changed. And it was getting excellent reviews. New images appeared on the screens: bright-orange background with the lines from a poet, dead now for some twenty years: *our flags in tatters, with and without wind, no fire left in our hearts.* She'd befriended him years ago. *Take water with you / the future will be dry.*

And the attention was international. The BBC did a feature on her, and the footage of Nefeli and the male British reporter walking through the megaphones was spliced into the video footage too. The European papers had all mentioned her show, including her absence at the opening, and all this both enraged the Greeks (why does *she* get all the foreign attention?) and filled them with pride (she's one of ours!).

One evening I rode home with the same taxi driver I'd had when I first arrived in Athens, when he first dropped me off at the apartment. This was not so unusual, but it felt, somehow, momentous. He recognized me and was talkative. The name of my street translates to "Of Warriors and Thieves"—*Armatolon kai Klefton*. The word for "sinners" is close to the word for "warriors"—just the transposing of two consonants—and I think even those who knew their history, that the *armatoloi kai kleftoi* were key figures during Ottoman rule, seemed to mishear it. The taxi driver asked me if I was a sinner, and I repeated the street. Yes, yes, he said. I know. But "sinners" rolls off the tongue faster. I forced a laugh.

The driver, maybe hearing my accent, told me he'd lived many years in New York and completely reinvented himself there, and when he returned to Athens he had to do it all over again.

I understood this need for reinvention. My father had done so brilliantly. My mother could not, but her old self could also not exist in the new place. For a while, I think, those first years in the United States, my mother was fighting something, on the verge of escape: from her body, from her mind. And somewhere in there, between the time I was five and twelve, she surrendered, began to damage her body as if to kill that other self. And when my teen years arrived, she began to sense a wildness in me, a desire to get out, go up, move away. She began to see that I had a *body* too. And if she did not feel outright hate, it was resentment,

151

and I don't know which is worse. She left Greece because she had felt she had to, whereas she saw my leaving home as a choice—and that offended her, just the way my changing body offended her. I didn't tell all this to the driver, of course, but I told it later that night, to the Captain.

There was a lot of traffic, and the taxi driver concentrated on the road. We drove the rest of the way home in silence, save for his taking a few calls. When we pulled up to my building he looked at me in his rearview mirror. "You're Greek," he asked. "Right?"

I didn't bother with "Greek American." Obviously, he figured this. I thanked him and got out of the car. He told me to take care of myself.

When I was growing up in Chicago it was not unusual for people to ask: *What are you?* They wanted your ethnic identity, and I never thought much of it; where I grew up, we were all from somewhere else, so the question was more curious than critical. But there was an element of racism to it. Here, I'd done it myself on the metro, seen teenagers of most likely Chinese or Nigerian heritage, say, and first thinking they were American tourists until I heard them speaking Greek with the mannerisms and gestures of native-born speakers, until I realized they *were* mostly likely native speakers. And I've seen people try to place Fady's origins. Asking about his name, where he went to school, puzzled at his elegant, refined Greek. He studied in Paris, he always says; he grew up there. It's not that he is rejecting his past, it's that he re-sists this quiet aggression, that somehow he owes people his story, owes them one solid, unchanging identity. He feels both Greek and not-Greek, he speaks Greek, and that is enough.

Me, I don't know what I felt. I didn't not feel Greek. I did not feel particularly American either, but I felt comfortable in my outsiderness. Maybe this was a function of Americanness, or whiteness, to feel one can go anywhere and belong. I certainly didn't feel Greek American. In Chicago I'd associated this only with church and Greek school. After my mother witnessed me, at a rehearsal, commemorate a historical event that involved clutching our dolls and falling to our deaths, she became enraged. "I don't want the village to follow me," she said, and I was yanked out before I had had the chance to jump from the stage, an act to which I had really been looking forward. When we got home she took a washcloth and vigorously scrubbed all the makeup off my face. My mother, so anxious that she might be rejected, was always the one to reject first. She and Nefeli were a lot alike.

I asked her once, after a discussion with my friends—all of us with immigrant parents, or immigrants ourselves, Ukrainian and Lebanese and Indian and Korean—if we were white. She answered without hesitation, *No*, she said, as if I were an idiot. *We're Greek.* She was begging the question but I dropped it.

"I could spend the rest of my life trying to understand her," I told the Captain.

"Have you ever written about her?" he asked.

I told him I'd only written about people who'd explicitly given me permission. People I came to know under the pretext of writing about them. As I said it I felt a little uneasy.

He was quiet for a moment. "So you don't *really* come to know them. Only who they're showing themselves to be."

I put my head down in my hands, suddenly dizzy, lightheaded. I could no longer be a cipher for other people's stories—not in the academic context. It was too difficult to not acknowledge how I changed the space. Even listening is not passive, but it's not as though I'd show up and listen. I spent weeks, months, years, even, building relationships. When I finished the oral histories, the most interesting things were the things I remembered, those things that had passed between us: a glance of knowing between the two of us, the long process of establishing friendship and trust, the moments spent laughing and crying. A hand held, a political fight, an inappropriate crush, a surprising loss. Those were the things I wanted to write. I did not mention my own parents, also who lived through the junta, who married when it was over, had me, and, five years later, left Greece for good.

I am certainly not the first to have had this feeling, but it has begun to weigh on me. My dissertation involved collecting oral histories from the junta, and my first book specifically the stories of women, from prison camp survivors to sympathizers of the regime. I am happy I wrote it. But compiling all these stories, arranging them, editing them—it was more art than scholarship. It's why I was so thrilled when Svetlana Alexievich won the Nobel for Literature, an acknowledgment that imagination was as much a part of what we did than what a novelist does, an acknowledgment of living with all those voices, a human ear, she called herself, carrying them with her.

The cicadas were loud but the neighborhood felt still, hot, like we were the only two people moving, in action. "Isn't that how we come to know anyone," I finally said. The wall between our balconies, which had allowed a kind of intimacy, at that moment felt cruel. I wanted him to put his hand on my shoulder, I wanted to see his eyes.

"Could be," he said.

"I wouldn't know where to start, writing about my mother."

"Haven't you already. Started."

"I guess. Yeah." I wished him goodnight, but instead of going to sleep, I went out, wandered through Exarcheia a while, feeling broken, tender to the entire city, as if she—all of her—were talking to me.

*

Since Nefeli's show had opened, she had stopped putting herself together. If I phoned while she was sleeping she became irritable. If I didn't phone she was more irritable still. She'd work and work and then disappear to the island, cut off communication, as if she needed to re-grow or reconstitute herself.

She wasn't eating properly and seemed to have a dry, incessant cough. Yet she talked about returning to yoga, or taking up running. These things she uttered with such conviction that I think she truly believed she might. The city, the protests, the bleak situation for the refugees, all things she cared about deeply—it was all becoming too much. The crisis was disappearing from the global panic stage but not in Greece itself, she said. How is this going to define us all, she wanted to know.

The crisis imaginary, she called it.

One afternoon, Dimitra and Fady and I went to visit her. When we arrived, she didn't look well but rushed us out of the flat. We asked if she'd eaten and she lied and said yes. But that day, she seemed eager to go out. Dimitra suggested a nearby old, traditional taverna Nefeli loved—my father had loved it too, and as a toddler I had often come here with my parents, my small stroller parked outside. In fact, there's a picture of me standing on a chair in a green dress on my third birthday, a paper crown on my head, my parents behind me, laughing. Nefeli had been a regular there since before I was born, the first public place she'd eaten when she returned from her island exile, barely nineteen. Maybe afterward I'd get her to lie down.

"No," she said. "It's a winter place." I knew it was something more. Instead she suggested a vegetarian restaurant in Syntagma, run by a young Greek woman and her Afghan husband—friendly, relaxed, impossibly thin, glowy yoga people who always spoke in generous, warm tones. It was a great place indeed, but far, and the metro was on strike and it was too hot to walk, and Nefeli refused, for whatever reason, to move through the city in a taxi. We went instead to a small Cretan place down the block.

Outside, a bag of trash had spilled onto the sidewalk. Nefeli swore, kicked a carton of juice down the street, and her foot became entangled with a plastic bag. A young man passing by us gave her a dirty look, his lip in a sneer.

I motioned for Fady and Dimitra to sit. He grabbed a table and Nefeli, without resistance, followed. She put her head down in her hands. "Nothing is changing," she said. Her voice was muffled, desperate. Fady glanced at me, quickly, and my gut tightened. He pointed toward the board, set up on the sidewalk: LOCALLY SOURCED. LOCAL DRINKS. VEGETARIAN.

"I mean. Seriously," he said.

I downed my draft before the first plates of food came—dakos salad, mini pies stuffed with mizithra cheese, fries—and ordered another, glancing at Fady and Nefeli to see if they'd noticed. I fidgeted with my phone.

"If you take a photo of this," Dimitra said, waving her hand over the table, "I swear I will get up and leave." I don't think I have ever posted a photo of a meal, but I said nothing. Nefeli, however, laughed, and we were all grateful for this. Fady rolled a cigarette and said if they made the sidewalk seating nonsmoking he'd riot. He rarely smoked. Nefeli stood to say hello to a friend inside then disappeared to the bathroom, stalking past a table of young people who stopped to watch her back disappear into the door. She was upsetting even the anarchists.

I waited for Fady to say something about the hipsterfication of this neighborhood, about crisis tourism, but he was quiet.

But he watched me closely, as if I might reveal something new. Did he think I knew something about Nefeli? Did he think I was drinking too much? Were we all watching one another this closely?

Meanwhile, Dimitra watched Nefeli, who was inside, talking with the bartender. The more distant a person, the less they knew about her, the more she lit up. When Nefeli returned to our table, Fady gently joked with her, and though she was usually quick-witted and acerbic, she didn't say much.

We paid our tab and Fady left for the workshop to meet a client. He sounded exhausted. He was worried about Rami's new-found moodiness, and Nefeli's unsettledness had us all in a constant state of unease. Dimitra headed to the squat, and Nefeli and I walked together. She asked if she could come to my place, sit on the balcony a moment. It was too hot for the balcony, where my laundry hung and dried within minutes, but I agreed. Even without air conditioning, my apartment's relative cool darkness felt nice. I turned on the ceiling fan, remembering how cold I'd been when I'd first arrived.

For a while, she stared, like a cat, through the pass-through into the living room. Finally, she lay down on the couch and fell asleep. I felt calm with her there, as though I was somehow protecting her. So much of my life Nefeli had looked out for me.

When I heard a thud, something falling to the ground, I checked in on her, but it was just her phone, having slipped from her pocket. I'd since hung some other paintings I'd found in the closet, her others from this series—the church on the island—and she napped underneath dark colors, each with shocks of Aegean blue. It was on a visit when I was fifteen that I made the connection between these images and Nefeli, a connection even now difficult to retain. Other paintings, those of the women, I kept in the closet, worried somehow that they'd upset her. But this is not why it's difficult for me to integrate these paintings of the young artist Nefeli with the woman who came to check on me when I arrived, the woman I drink beer with at Mavili. When you know somebody so well, it's hard to also recognize their public selves. I see Aris's name now in the paper, the rising star of his party, and I read it with both detached fascination and a knot in my gut. Even I, the person who writes the oral histories, who publishes the essays, is not the same self who now writes these words. She is barely here at all.

Nefeli's show, her insistence on both a retrospective and new work, was part of her desire to define time as anything that was not *now*: yesterday, tomorrow, last year. Her anger that day was a sort of premonition, a glimpse into a future we didn't want to see. Or a future we could see but had no power to alter.

In the early evening Nefeli woke and I made some tea—she drank it with milk and honey, which is how I now drank it, even in summer—and when I returned to the table with the tray she was staring at the painting, as if she had not noticed it before. I waited for her to say something but she didn't. We drank our tea and she suggested a walk.

We headed down along Lykavittos, and Nefeli was quiet until we reached the entrance of the park. "I forgot you had those others," she said. "The paintings."

I hoped it didn't rekindle bad feelings: about Haroula, other loves, a past that was never really past. She was indeed in another conversation. "There are so many ways to be unfaithful," she continued. "There are so many ways to betray someone."

We walked through the park, where the keening of the cicadas was almost deafening; they were trapped in their own nightmare. She stopped walking, to listen. "They're dying," she said. "That's why they sing." She kissed me on both cheeks. "I'm going home now," she said, and when she disappeared around the corner I had a sickening feeling I would not see her again.

In some way, I was right.

Back in my apartment I detected the faint smell of rosewater, like my mother used to wear. I couldn't look at Nefeli's paintings. I sat in the living room and tried to read, but found myself turning pages without having taken in a word.

Nearby, someone's rock band had begun to practice, their piercing guitars filling the courtyard with a Metallica song I remembered from my childhood, which soon transitioned to a heavy metal version of "Evdokia's Zeibekiko," which I also remember from my childhood. My mother had wanted to name me Evdokia, after the movie, and my father was incensed because the character was a prostitute. Since the film, no one could have that name without association, he said, though I thought it was a great name, meaning "she whose deeds are good." Instead, they named me Myrto, and often called me the diminutive, Myroula. When we moved to Chicago, both versions proved difficult for English speakers, and I became Mira. But in Greek, it sounds like the word "fate," a name that seems to ask for trouble, and my parents rarely used it, and Nefeli never did. Me, I answered to both.

A few mornings later, I went down for my mail. In the foyer next to the mailboxes was a large box inscribed with my name, not shipped but simply dropped off. I opened it up and found several new pairs of lacy underwear in light, springy colors, wrapped in tissue paper; a pile of Greek poetry books translated into English; a stack of old Greek postcards from the 1970s; and a new box of notecards, printed with Nefeli's early paintings, the kind you'd find in a museum gift shop; and two packages of Thassian olives. She'd opened the box of notecards and used one, of the print that hung in my living room, to write: *For Myrto xo N.* I called to thank her but she didn't pick up her phone, so I sent a text: *Thank you, dear Nefeli. What is all this for?*

She wrote a few hours later. *Just a little gift.*

That night, the garbage strike ended, and when the trucks barreled down the narrow streets of the neighborhood, I stood with Sophia outside her shop. People clapped and cheered and the drivers waved, like a postwar parade. I looked up to the Captain's front balcony, where he stood watching as well. He waved at us both. "Ah ha," Sophia said.

Fady began a new cello he'd deliver to a musician in Berlin.
He planned to spend some time with friends, working on another sound project, though I knew he wouldn't be able to leave
Rami, who was going with him, right away. The details and the
timing were confusing. Fady kept it quiet, and I knew to stop
asking, knowing that he'd had to arrange something convolut-
ed and questionable and even that would take a while. Though
Rami talked about his brother often, he never said a word about
Germany, as if it, and his future there, did not yet exist. Then
again, I could not imagine Athens without him, and I, too, didn't
want to see this future, which to me also did not exist.

That day, the building and the courtyard were oddly still. I
stood on my balcony. I wondered what the Captain was doing.
I knew he was leaving soon, and he seemed to become a little
distant, withdrawn, or maybe it was me. I didn't leave the house
for two days. Dimitra texted from Syntagma: there was another
parliamentary vote about to happen, but at this point it felt as
if the papers could simply have run the last story that appeared
about it. Trapped in a cycle.

At the squat that week a small girl, the one whose hand Rami
had held at the eye doctor's, glued herself to my side when I
taught. Though she was three, perhaps even four, she did not
speak. Her father was there with her, though I had never seen
him; many of the men were not around while we were. She listened and nodded, and in the English lessons I could tell she
was learning the words. She would point out the photos when I
would say *cat* or *water* or *house*. She drew houses, again and again.
One day, some of the volunteers outside the classroom were playing with the other children, making paper crowns. She came in

to show me and I said, *Crown!* And she nodded, so proud, and pointed to my phone. We took a photo. Rami loved her, too, and when he spoke to her in Arabic she beamed. When I asked Rami if she spoke to him, he said no, she hadn't said a word since she arrived. He drew her pictures—a frog, a house, a field of flowers—and she'd march around the courtyard with them, proud. She'd sit down with some crayons, coloring in the lines. Rami always let her paint his nails.

After, I took Rami back to Dimitra and Fady's. Dimitra and I sat in her kitchen, having coffee. "Do you think Rami wants to stay *here*," I asked. "With you and Fady and Leila. Go to the American school in the fall."

"He has relatives in Germany."

"I know. But not his parents."

"Well. His brother. His father's cousin, her husband. Still, *family.*"

I didn't say anything.

Dimitra hit the table with her hand. "For fuck's sake, Mira," she said. "We can't just *take* the kid. He doesn't belong to everyone. He's not mine, he's not Fady's, Leila is not his sister."

But Leila was like a sister. To me, they *were* a family. "Okay. I'm sorry. I didn't mean to upset you. Was just thinking aloud."

"Sometimes you're so first-world. So *white*. You think you have a solution to everything."

"You haven't thought of it?" I recalled Fady's excitement when Rami watched soccer with him, which Leila had long outgrown. The way they'd all watch movies together on the big couches, piled under blankets, Fady's special popcorn.

"Enough," Dimitra said. "Change the subject, please."

When I came home I felt as though I had forgotten something, and as I pushed open my door I remembered: the Captain was leaving, headed for the island with his family for the summer. "For the kids," he'd said a few nights ago as we spoke on the balcony, as if I deserved an explanation. "Katerina took them out of school early," he added, in case I was wondering. They were returning to Greece. His wife had a few weeks of vacation and would accompany them initially, but when she returned to Brussels he'd stay with the kids on the island.

I hurried home, bounded up the steps, and went out to the balcony and listened. Stuck on my side of the partition were a few Post-it notes, as if he had reached his arm around and placed them there.

Mira. I have to go. Talk soon.

The second one had his phone number. I still had the yellow pad on which he'd written it the first time, in the top drawer of my desk, a remnant from that first, early encounter with the heater that now felt like a surreal offering, rewritten by the contract between us.

The third: *??????!* Strength. This one was written in a different-colored pen, and then he included a goofy smiley face, which seemed delightfully out of character. I went inside and stuck all three on the wall atop my desk. I sat down hard in the chair. My lip was trembling.

But only minutes later came a knock on the door. You had to be buzzed in to the building, so no one knocked except the woman on the second floor who got angry when we didn't lock the building door from the inside at night, or the superintendent who came to collect the payment for the shared utilities—but she had come by two days earlier. Nefeli always let herself in, too, but she always announced herself, slightly irritated. *Myrto let me in.*

It was the Captain. He wore jeans and a navy T-shirt. Rubber sandals, the type soccer players wear. An old duffel bag at his side. Light beard. New glasses, dark red. I smiled. I so rarely saw him in person, and this glimpse into his wardrobe warmed my heart. I could hardly connect him to the person I spoke with in that precarious safety of the balcony.

"I was loading my car but wanted to check once more if you were home."

"New glasses," I said. So strange to do so watching his facial expressions, seeing his body language, as I spoke. He smiled.

"Do you want to have a beer?" As though I invited him in every evening.

He hesitated. "I'm sorry." He drew the words out. "I have to go."

He looked down at me, breathed in. Then he placed his hand on my head, as if in benediction. "Be good," he said. He moved his hand through my hair, first as if he'd gone to playfully tousle it but reconsidered midmotion. It was an awkward moment, but then he continued running his hand through its length, slowly, tangles and all. A pleasant shiver ran down the back of my neck, my spine.

He brought his hand to my cheek, tapped my nose. "You got some sun," he said.

I touched my nose and smiled. My words were lodged in my throat. "See you," I said.

13

The Captain

Katerina and the kids returned from Brussels and I rejoined them in Kifissia. Those several days before we left for the island, we didn't discuss a legitimate split. Katerina was not wavering, but I suspect she feared the judgment of her friends and her parents, and perhaps also the unknown. In no hurry to go through with anything official, she accepted the odd, indeterminate state between us. Though sometimes it frustrated me, other times I gladly accepted it. There was a renewed affection between us, and we even had sex far more often than we had in years.

Then one night, afterward, she emerged from the bathroom in a pair of white pajamas and T-shirt: "This doesn't mean we shouldn't proceed with the divorce," she said. We had not yet used the word, but she now spoke of divorce the way others might have discussed a long vacation, a new house—something exciting in the indefinite future.

She got into bed beside me and asked if I regretted anything. I asked her where I should start. She laughed. But though I would never tell her that the marriage, this life, was never what I had envisioned for myself, I could not imagine another reality, not really.

When I asked her the same, though, her face turned serious. "Regret," she said. "I regret regret."

I stared at the ceiling fan, and she sat back up and scrolled through her phone. A friend from Brussels had sent her some photos, which she showed me. One close-up captured her profile. She was laughing, a raucous, full-body laugh, and I felt a pang of sadness, knowing that I could never give her such joy. I commented how happy and young she looked, and she smiled. I didn't ask who had taken the photo, or who waited on the other end of the message. In another life I would ask who had sent it, but I no longer had the right.

It's a horrible feeling, to be with one person but thinking of another.

I lay there staring at the ceiling. There had been something in her motions, her body, the way she pitched her hips up toward me as we had sex, that had felt new, unfamiliar. Something unsettling, even haunting, about the entire act.

It made one thing clear: she was still in love. Just not with me.

Later, I sat on the balcony of our bedroom, which overlooked our green street stretching ahead in front of me, widening as it ascended the hill before it dipped down into a small square that contained a large fountain and two lively cafés. Katerina poked her head outside and startled me. "I'm going to sleep," she said.

"Me too."

But I stalled, read a bit of a novel. When I finally got into bed Katerina turned to face me. "I worry about you alone, without us to tether you." She intertwined her smooth, cold feet in mine, and we fell asleep together. How can anyone possibly understand what goes on in a marriage? How can anyone put it to language?

I woke in the middle of the night to what I recognized as the long, lamenting blast of a ship's foghorn, but I was not near the sea, and this was impossible.

The next morning I dressed in the shaky early light and went for a run. The park was fuller than I remember it being on Saturday mornings. Everyone had, all at once, taken up running, then stayed in these clothes all day long. Athens looked like a Nike ad. I used to see the former prime minister running here, in expensive running gear and a gaggle of security. Mira had told me she'd seen the current prime minister running through Lykavittos, with two men and a woman in old sweatpants and T-shirts, and they'd smiled and waved at her. I came across the bend on a lesser-run trail and frightened a couple whose posture signaled they were either fighting or guilty. They looked at me as though I'd discovered them. I apologized and kept going.

I ran much longer than usual.

I knew I could not keep up this duality much longer, and when I returned to the house I'd tell Katerina I would go to the island but stay at my father's during the time she was there. When she went back to Brussels, I'd stay there with the kids so they wouldn't have to leave.

When I came home, the twins asked me how many turtles I'd seen in the park, and I lied and told them three. I hadn't paid attention. I decided against my earlier idea. They all looked so happy. Katerina, still in her white pajamas, made pancakes. I walked to the massive refrigerator and filled my glass with ice, making a clownish show of it, acting surprised as all the ice tumbled to the floor.

Katerina looked up absentmindedly, and Ifigenia asked, "What is wrong with you?" before they realized I was trying to make them laugh.

*

The night before we left for the island, I overhead a bit of Katerina's phone conversation with her sister Effie. They were talking about the EU, in which Katerina was adamant about Greece's staying.

"Who knows what will happen without the EU," Katerina said. "Without the euro. We go back to the drachma?"

It was clear from Katerina's responses that Effie disagreed. So many Greeks wanted to try something new. End the suffering already.

You see? I don't blame anyone. But in a way, I do.

I was watching television alone in the den when Katerina reappeared and said they were all going to the movies. Normally she'd have invited me to join, but we had settled quietly into a new normal: separate lives underneath one roof. She asked if I wanted her to bring me something to eat but I said I'd be fine.

I was not used to being alone in this space; I even missed their noise. A few buildings over, someone held a party, the balcony adorned with white Moroccan lights. I thought of Morocco, leaving it, passing the Canary Islands, so bright and colorful they felt like a storybook.

On another balcony a couple kissed; nearby some small children played with trucks while an older man, their grandfather, smoked a cigarette and scrolled through his phone. A cat stared at me, wanting something. I felt uneasy, exposed, yet deeply embedded in my loneliness, its haunting presence. I missed the sea. I went back inside and turned on the television, but every channel I turned to featured people shouting at one another, or miserable. Others just showed what seemed an endless string of loud car-chase scenes. I felt anxious and turned it off.

It was only about twenty minutes after everyone had left for the movies that I grabbed my keys and was out the door, driving to the center of the city. When I pulled into my apartment building's underground parking, I felt my insides swerve. I bought a beer from Sophia, who grinned at me as though betraying involvement in some sort of secret plot. I let myself in, walked across the old floors still wearing my shoes. I opened up the windows to the early evening.

I drank my beer on the balcony, waiting.

And waiting. I went to Sophia and bought another bottle. She was talking to the man who owned the karate place down the way, so I was able to come in and out without interrogation. I went back upstairs and settled back onto the balcony. There was no telling how long I could wait, or what, really, I was waiting for. For all I knew Mira was out of town, or sleeping at a new boyfriend's; maybe she'd decided to go to the island, too. Athens was becoming unbearably hot.

If she did show up, now, I'd have to leave anyway. Saturday night traffic: it would take me a while to get back to Kifissia. I'd already pushed my luck. If Katerina was home with the kids before I was, I'd just tell them I went to the local taverna for dinner.

On my way out of the building I ran right into Nefeli. Though I'd attended her exhibit, I hadn't seen her in years. I still thought of her the way she'd been when *I'd* been a teenager, she in her late twenties. I'd met her often in Athens with my father. There's one time in particular that still stands out, the marks of forced exile all over her face. It was winter. Back then, her black hair was longer than any woman's I'd ever seen, and she wore a thick white turtleneck sweater, a thick headband. All those big layers made her look tiny, fragile, but she had smiled at me, grabbed my cheek. "Does your mother know you're out?" she asked. She'd called me "little captain" before I was even a captain, but my grandfather had also been a captain and had felt betrayed, I think, by my father's move to politics. Perhaps I chose it, unconsciously, as a sort of atonement for the sins of my father. My father, of course, took it—took everything—as a slight.

"Have you seen our Myrto today," she asked.

I had never heard anyone use her Greek name. "Not today," I said. *Unfortunately.*

"I need something from her place," she said. "But I have a key," she added. She'd lived here for years, after all.

"How's my father," I asked. Despite having spent nearly a week on the island, I hadn't managed to see him. Minas had assured me he was fine, staying at Nefeli's cabin on the mountain. I had assumed he was with her, but now here she was.

She looked particularly vulnerable and I felt a rush of tenderness toward her. "Oh, he's fine," she said, but I didn't believe her. I think she must have realized this because she asked if I understood what was happening to him. "His mind, it's not the same. But we understand one another. We share the same fears," she said.

"The same fears," I repeated, hoping she'd elaborate. She didn't. I told her I was going to the island again, this time for the summer. She said she was returning soon as well. And probably not coming back.

"Until winter?"

"Not coming back," she said.

I didn't know what to say, so I waited for her to speak again. Her comments had rattled me. "Oh, don't worry about him," she said at last. "It's only melancholia." Then she tipped her head, as if trying to see me from a different angle. "What is it that defines you?" she asked.

I didn't know what she was talking about, and when I hesitated she waved her hand between us, as if dismissing what hung there. When I hugged her goodbye I could feel her delicate bones beneath her sleeveless black shirt, like the tiny bones of a quail.

Driving home, Nefeli's question loomed large in my mind. Two things, for many years, have defined me as a man: the sea and my marriage. As imperfect as my relationship with Katerina has been—though I do believe that the definition of a relationship is imperfect; it was something I'd read somewhere when I was a student and had returned to the island after a painful breakup—I did not know who I would be without her. Take my life at sea out of the equation and I was an empty shell, needing reconstitution. But with what materials? Who was I before Katerina? Before the sea? I'd have to go so far back as university, studying litera-ture, the pleasure of the language, the young guy who kicked the soccer ball along the beach while the young Aris watched, both of us dreaming of what might lie ahead. Yet I studied engineering anyway, then returned for my military service, and the navy. So instead of disappearing into words, I escaped into the sea, a different place of the imagination. And now I seemed to be escaping again—not to the sea but away from it.

The apartment, then, which I'd previously seen as an escape, a liminal space between my domestic life in Kifissia and my solitary life at sea, had become the place I'd begun to redefine myself. I'd come to love it the way I loved that island village where my father has made his home, a place I'd never felt landlocked but instead as if I were soaring above the earth.

And somehow this had to do with Mira. That night, as I was falling asleep, it occurred to me with a sort of urgency that the balcony was not the venue for our intimacy. The balcony, that space, had become the intimacy itself, allowing us to be two things, to occupy two places, at once. The meeting in the *metaxi*, the in-between, the what-if. It was a limbo, but one in which I strangely felt whole in the split.

*

We reached the island just after noon. Usually the kids were anxious to swim, but today they were moody and inconsolable. Ifigenia had refused to pack her bag at home, and Katerina, exasperated and knowing we'd miss the boat, did it for her. Nikos texted his friends the entire time, wanting to continue some video game they played together online. I didn't know there was such a thing, and when I mentioned that to Katerina, she looked startled that such important details of his life I had only just now realized.

The house near the port had been purchased by my father years ago for me and my brother, with the plan that each of us would spend as much time as we could there with our families. Though neither of us had a great relationship with him, it pained him that we, his sons, were not closer with each other. My father's house in the village couldn't accommodate all the children, nor was it near the water where they always wanted to be. However, since my brother never visited Greece, the house felt like ours.

When we arrived, we went through the usual rituals: refilling the refrigerator with groceries from the port, putting the fresh towels in the bathroom and the sheets on the bed. There was a particular smell to the island house—stone and sea and small lavender soaps shaped like seashells that sat in a dish next to shells the twins had collected—evoking in me such wild nostalgia that I decided I would need to leave sooner than I had anticipated.

The kids were in their room, getting ready to go to the beach. I told them I needed to see my father, that I was going to stay with him. I felt ashamed; they were not idiots. Of course they knew that their parents' marriage was not a normal one, and their sad, downturned lips broke my heart. "Okay, Dad," they said.

I hugged Katerina at the door.

When I told her several days ago that I felt it best if I stayed at my father's until she returned to Brussels, we'd fought. There would be no way to forestall the conversation with the children, which she feared would ruin their summer. And I felt torn, of course, wanting to do what was best for them. Yet the minute I'd seen the island come into view from the bow of the ferry, I knew

I couldn't do it. It would be too painful. In Athens, I had learned to live my split lives. But not here.

Yet the emotion I felt at the moment was less sadness than shame. Ashamed because I had assumed my half-presence in Katerina's life would be enough, ashamed that I had failed. And devastated because I did love her, and if she had been giving me clues to try to repair the marriage, as she claimed, I had missed them. I had let her down, just as I'd let down all the others. To continue this attachment was purely prolonging what had to come.

I suppose my father stayed with Nefeli because he was lonely, but it was unbearable to imagine my father's loneliness. According to Nefeli, he liked to be around her while she created something. His bees were just down the road from her cottage, and she said that sometimes, when she was working, she'd stand on her roof and see him down there, moving slowly with his beekeeper hat and gloves, going about his routine. He'd begun making beeswax candles, brewing honey wine, gardening. So many things I could not imagine.

My father asked me to meet him at Thanassis's, but when I arrived he was not there, which was not unlike him. My father not only expected me to come to him but also to wait, even when he was young and I was overwhelmed with the twins. But now, he was difficult to find. When was the last time I'd actually seen him? The past year for me was a blur.

I was not meeting with my father for any sort of reckoning; I did not expect to suddenly shift our relationship. Once it's solidified in its habits, which it had, years and years ago, we can only hope for its best possible version. But as I'd walked from my car to the center of the village, I decided I'd tell him Katerina and I were splitting. Otherwise, he'd wonder why I wasn't staying with them, and I surely didn't want him to think I thought he needed supervision. Did he?

Whether as buffer, foil, or insurance in case he decided not to show up, my father had invited Minas to join us. He welcomed me, poured me some raki, offered me some little marinated fish. Minas lived in the village in the winter but fished in the warmer months, when he lived in a small house, nearly a shack, not far from the shore. I had hoped he'd give me greater insight into my father, his recent behavior, but like many others of his generation they refused to speak of such things, a sort of self-preservation of dignity to not disclose the wreckage of aging. My chest felt tight, and I don't know if it was anger or a bruised tenderness or something in between.

"What's wrong with you?" Minas asked.

I didn't answer, of course. I felt tense. I remembered what Mira had said about my father, about consciousness and memory as the story of a self, even if the story seems muddled or confusing.

"Your father is coming, don't worry," Minas said, and this affection, this man of his generation covering for him, smoothing over his forgetfulness, broke my heart. But soon my father indeed appeared, in dark jeans and a light denim shirt, his thick hair combed back like an actor's, cigarettes in his front shirt pocket. He had a tan and wore a beard, which he hadn't in years. He looked startlingly handsome.

I stood, and I was surprised that my father hugged me, and tightly. He was an affectionate man overall, but rarely with me. Not since I'd been a boy. It's as though he was forgetting his habits, his resentments, his way of being in the world. "You look good," I said.

He pulled at his shirt collar. "A gift from Nefeli," he said, beaming.

Minas called him a handsome fucker and my father said: "Well, at least I still have my looks." His expression clouded for a moment, but then they both broke into laughter, the two of them laughing as though it were the funniest thing in the world.

*

Later, when I told my father about Katerina, he had not reacted the way I'd expected. Instead, he put his hand on my arm and asked if I was okay, if I needed anything. He asked if he could call Katerina and I said yes, of course. I slept at his house that night, and he did too, following me into my room and talking to me awhile at the edge of the bed, like he might have done once or twice when I was a child. I woke in the night to hear him through the wall, talking in his sleep, long paragraphs I could not decipher, as if he were giving a speech.

The next evening, I went to see the kids and Katerina for dinner. After, the twins had gone with friends to the outdoor cinema a few blocks away, so we were alone. I told Katerina my father was no longer a man I recognized. He was a different person. But to himself, he was the self he always was; I don't think he recognized the difference. Her lip quivered, and she burst into tears. I followed her into the bathroom, where she sat atop the toilet seat, and I put my hand on her head. "Don't worry," I said. "He'll be okay." Katerina had always loved him,

I knew. She hugged her face to my hip. "I know," she said. "It's not that."

I sat down on the floor, my feet up on the tub's ledge. "I need to see where this goes," she said. "I will regret it if I don't." At first I thought she was talking about us, about our marriage, and my heart soared. But then I realized she was talking about someone, something, else. She curled into me, and we stayed like that awhile. Finally, she stood up, washed her face, and I knew it was time for me to go. It was then that she said, "I wish it could all be more—I don't know. I wish it could all be more." She kept apologizing, and I could see she was in deep pain, but mostly I knew that the pain was because I, somehow, had abandoned her first.

14

Mira

We woke to the news of the vandalism. Fady called early in the morning to tell me the story, which was not much of a story but simply an event, a series of details that he kept repeating as if some sense might arise from their recitation. Over the night, vandals had destroyed the megaphone installation, those outside the museum and the few around the city. I insisted we go have a look, try to clean it up. Nefeli, of course, didn't respond to our calls or messages.

We went anyway, Fady and Dimitra and I. A crowd of young people had already gathered, wanting to clean it up, to restore it. The long line of megaphones that lined the walkway headed to the museum, that circled the entrance, had been kicked in, holes punched through, covered with graffiti. The cameras, interestingly, had not been disturbed, though it had happened in the middle of the night and they were not on.

Dimitra told them to wait, to see what Nefeli wanted. They all stopped what they were doing and looked at us as if we were all crazy. I'm sure when we'd turn away they'd shoot photos of themselves there, their smooth-skinned faces lighting up each other's screens. One woman—dyed black hair, heavy boots, velvet leggings despite the heat, the rest of her slight, sweet looking——asked if she was sure, said that Nefeli was allowing herself to be silenced.

"Let it be, please," Dimitra said.

"But what about expression," another asked.

"Expression," Dimitra said, the register of her voice shifting, as if Nefeli were speaking through her. "Whose expression?" As if the first time hearing the words, trying them out on her tongue. "Is that what you think art is for?"

*

Nefeli sold five new paintings, just like that. The vandalism had given her new street cred. Oddly enough, all this had temporarily invigorated her, given her work another element, another chapter. But none of us saw her. She responded to texts, but sporadically. Yet she was aware of the attention. She did a radio interview, and one of the arts-and-culture magazines wrote a feature on her, but she refused to appear in public. Fady spliced some of her interview comments into the soundscape. Her voice, disembodied this way, was eerier than I could ever have imagined:

Art is not about expression. Art is about porousness.

And the one that killed me: *Art is a conversation with the dead.*

I went with some friends to the taverna, the one with the chandelier that had hung in Tito's home, beneath the painting by the Serbian artist Nefeli had known. The owner recognized me and asked if I'd seen her. I wished I'd had better news.

Her disappearance made me feel as though I were fading too. Midafternoons I'd open a beer and fall asleep again until evening. I missed the Captain. I missed being invisible yet seen, the feeling of being so alive in my body but yet not of the body at all. What a relief it was sometimes to be not-looked-at, to feel my edges sharpen again, less worn down by the gaze. I closed the shutters, with the urgent desire to disappear.

I wasn't getting any work done. And as for university business, I'd open my email and see a note from a colleague wanting to form some ad-hoc committee, or from students needing something. "Hey Mira," the notes began, if they addressed me at all. Though they referred, often in the same note, to my male colleagues as "Professsor." I'd close the email, my arms too heavy to type a response. I knew I was lucky to have this good position. I knew I should not take it for granted. It was as if my academic life in the States no longer existed or mattered. Yet I had the constant feeling I was forgetting something.

I'd sometimes wake late from a nap, make more coffee, and begin to write. Or attempt to. Then I'd be wired, so I'd have another drink. Some days the birdsong would be in the courtyard, the morning light graying the sky, by the time I'd be able to fall asleep. This repeated for several days, which blurred together.

But then one day Dimitra called at 12:30. I'd missed my class at the school, my tutoring with Rami. I apologized, told her I could make it there in an hour. She said not to bother.

She called again an hour later to ask, *Should I be concerned?*
"About?" I asked.

"This is the second class you missed this week."

The second? I pulled out my phone to check the calendar.

"Is everything alright, Mira?"

"It's nothing," I said. "Just a few bad days."

How much. How much does she drink.

I showed up the following afternoon to make up for the missed classes. Dimitra was also there, with Rami, who wouldn't look me in the eyes, but I could see him scanning my face when I looked away. Suddenly he'd become a teenager, shooting up several inches, his voice dropping an octave. "I'm sorry," I said. I wanted to make excuses—work, exhaustion, grief—but I knew what such apologies sounded like.

My mother called out to me from the cement bench inside the school's courtyard, where she smoked a cigarette and read the leftist paper. "You see what it feels like? Now you know."

I sat on a bench and scrolled through my phone. On a whim, I opened a message to the Captain. I'd entered his phone number after he scrawled it on the corner of a yellow legal pad on my small desk, from that day I'd asked him about the heater. I'd never used it, of course. When I wanted to talk I opened the door to the balcony. I typed and typed deleted and deleted, saying nothing, what to say, but something was compelling me to connect. Hi. Hello. *Ti kaneis. Ti yinetai.* Are you sleeping. I gave up. The instinct to tell him something was so visceral yet we had never really established this sort of communication. Besides those few occasions—the island, the roof—our chats were sequestered to the balcony and for now that's where they would stay. We had not established a pattern of public communication. We did not meet for coffee, and besides those few small interactions—a

brush of our bodies in the stairwell, his hand through my hair—
that loomed so large in my mind, we'd barely touched. Though
I did not exactly understand his marital situation, he seemed to
still have a marital situation, and I did not want to knock on that
door, not even in the spirit of friendship. Those conversations,
had I imagined them? They took on the quality of dreams so
vivid they broke the barrier of memory. The barrier of anything.

But Rami warmed to me, and we sat together on that same
bench where my mother had smoked her cigarette. He showed
me some more of his drawings, which were becoming more and
more sophisticated: kids with black-and-blue hair, long streets
lined with citrus trees, and the empty, blocked-out squares for
the rest of his story.

Everything felt either rigidly compartmentalized or limitless.

*

What happened after the vandalism was that a young collective of
artists, instead of cleaning up the graffiti and repairing the punc-
ture wounds in the megaphones, had stenciled them with blue
scorpions skittering into and out of the holes. When I walked to
the small square where many of them assembled, near the squat, I
found Leila there, her eyebrows dyed blue. She, too, was growing,
her face moving from a child's to a young woman's, an angularity
to her features she didn't have just few months ago.

She asked if I'd spoken with Rami. I said of course I had.
"Why?"

She looked at me, as if deciding what to say. "No reason,"
she said.

I asked if she'd seen Nefeli, and she shook her head.

The museum curator hadn't seen her either, and Nefeli, after those interviews, had refused to communicate any instructions regarding the installation. Her laconic, spare emails said the same thing she'd said originally: it was public space, it belonged to everyone and no one, that she'd had no right to it, that those vandals, and now the artists, had every bit of right that she did. It kept her narrative moving. Meanwhile, some of the local residents were complaining, wanting it cleaned up, didn't like all those kids hanging around. For all she knew, Nefeli said, they had been the culprits.

I went by Nefeli's apartment. She didn't answer the bell, but when another resident left I walked in like I belonged there. I was, after all, good at that. I knocked on her door, called to her gently, but there was nothing. Her neighbor heard me knocking and offered that several days before she'd seen her leaving with a duffel bag, her easel, her camera around her neck. Her mail was piled up in the foyer.

Fady and Dimitra hadn't seen her either. One night, Dimitra and I got drunk on my balcony, and she leaned in and asked, "Do you think Nefeli vandalized her own work?"

The possibility had not crossed my mind. "She likes attention," I said. "But not this much." Still, her comments stayed with me a long time. I understood something I don't think I had before: that Nefeli and her art were the same thing. That the same kinetic energy that went into her work could destroy her: she both created and absorbed it. Not a collection of selves but but a composite *I*. Whole.

Nefeli's show continued to run, and the vandalism gave it even more publicity. It was all over the art magazines, the culture pages. Dutch tourists were always being interviewed outside the museum. The screen displayed those scurrying scorpions and the young artists dressed in black, some still with blue eyebrows, streaks in their hair, juxtaposed with footage of protests in Syntagma, from the tent city that was there several years before. I couldn't free myself of the notion that Nefeli had somehow merged into her work. Time was folding in on itself. I took a photo of the screen and then of the installation outside.

That night I dreamt of those blue scorpions, vivid, graphic, scurrying, and I woke up hot, sweat pooling on my lower back, behind my neck. I drank a glass of water and washed my face, ran a cool washcloth over my skin. From the balcony I stared down on the courtyard. The moon was bright. In the distance the low bass beats from a club still sounded, a group of female voices laughed, a woman told a story she found so funny that she gasped to get the words out.

Are you there, I asked, to no one.

Back inside, I moved closer to Nefeli's painting and in the near darkness noticed something blue next to the figure of a woman, on the floor. I stared at it a long time, and its outlines seemed to sharpen. I had never paid attention to it before, but now in the dark I was sure it was a scorpion. In the corner, near the balcony door, my mother slept upright in my reading chair, her glasses resting on her chest.

When I woke up I returned to the painting. The blue was just a splash of color. Nothing more.

When I'd moved into this apartment it had felt nearly blank. I knew I had lived here and I had remembered certain moments: the way the window in the kitchen looked into another person's kitchen in the next building, the sound of the elevator, the wash of light in the living room in the morning, the violent spin of the washing machine, the echo of voices in the stairwell. But there had been something collapsed about it. The longer I stayed the longer I felt the web of interconnections filling it back with breath: me, my parents, the Captain, Nefeli, Haroula, Rami, Leila, Dimitra, Fady.

When I went down to check my mail—something I did religiously in Chicago but often would forget for days in Athens, as if I were somehow unreachable—I found a letter addressed to the Captain that had been mistakenly placed in my box. I held it in my hand like it was a small, delicate animal. I read his name out loud, acknowledging his identity as something far outside of myself, outside our intersections. I am unable to rectify his given name with the man who speaks to me, conversations so hushed and intimate they nearly feel like talks with myself.

Heavy sleep. Shadow dreams of Greek school. Morning rehearsals of a performance, cider and donuts, the only reason I liked to go. All the children were asked to come up to the stage, but I kept eating my French cruller, quite happily, and looking over at my mother, smiling at all the kids swarming to the front. Somehow I did not think I was one of them, and my mother waved me to go too, and I was alarmed. I climbed onto the stage, now my older self, walked past the children, and slipped through the heavy velvet curtain, which led me to my balcony, where the Captain waited for me.

15

Mira

When I came to Athens for my parents' burial I didn't make it to the island. Despite the shock of winter green, the bleak wind and stillness would have been too much. Now, my first trip back, the ferry moved through the mist like a phantom voyage. But within an hour the weather had cleared and I sat on the top deck, my face to the sun. For a short while I forgot myself and felt content.

Then, as the first island began to appear on the horizon, I felt a returning creep of dread. Five months earlier my parents were still alive. Four months earlier I'd still been with Aris, wandering through his Plaka apartment in a daze, comforted by his presence, his tenderness then. Eva would have already been pregnant. What had he told her? An old friend had come to stay? His girlfriend, in fact, but no, the timing was wrong for telling her?

From the island port, it's a fifteen-minute walk to the house. On the way was a small parking lot, and only then did I notice my parents' old flat-nosed Fiat. My mother drove that car all around the island, my father in the passenger seat, chatting. Most of the time, I only realize now, she was probably drunk, or well on her way.

To return to a place again and again is to confront the sneaky passing of time. Here I am at fifteen, at twenty-five, at twenty-nine, at thirty-nine. What of those earlier selves is left in me?

Our narrow street was deserted. I pulled my suitcase up the steep incline and climbed the stairs to our red front door. I don't know why, but I knocked. When I was a child I used to come to our own door and ask, in Greek, if the American girl could come out to play, and I think there was a part of me that hoped I would appear from the inside of the house, my own double. Now I hesitated under the stone archway, fumbled for the key, and let myself in.

What always hit me the hardest was the smell: the wool of the rugs that hung on the walls, the white flokati on the tile floor. When the place hadn't been aired out it smelled slightly of mold, which held a comforting familiarity, though Kyria Voula, who cared for me when I was a child, must have recently been by because the windows were open.

I opened drawers and cupboards. Whereas the flat in Athens had been mostly stripped of my parents, save for those few reminders, a few things in the storage closet, the memory of the rooftop, they were everywhere here. In the top-left cabinet I found the briki—my father only drank Greek coffee, and luckily there were plenty of places near our home in Chicago to indulge his particularly endearing snobbery—and the water glasses, the small blue tumblers for juice. On the other side stood the whiskey glasses, and behind them the plastic cups I used as a child. The other cupboard held my father's various bottles of tsipouro and behind them my mother's arsenal: vodka, bourbon, gin.

As I waited for coffee to boil, I opened the linen closet and put my face to a soft white pillowcase dotted with small blue flowers. Behind the clean towels I noticed some glass and retrieved an almost-empty whiskey bottle, as if my mother had told herself that if she didn't polish it off, she had barely had any at all.

I don't know why I thought I'd be alone in this house. I texted Nefeli, wondering if she were here, but got no response. Part of the reason I'd come to the island was to look for her. And partly because my apartment had felt so empty without my nightly conversations with the Captain.

Soon I collapsed onto my small double bed and didn't move for an hour, exhausted from all the grief that seemed to exponentially compound with each new event, each new addition. I wanted to empty myself of it.

I took a fresh towel from the closet and unwrapped an olive oil soap. In the mirror I saw the pattern from the woven blanket imprinted in my cheek. I forgot to first turn on the hot water heater, so I froze in the shower. Still, after, I felt a bit better, though the weight of all those physical reminders of loss had exhausted me.

Everything leaves its mark.

Fortunately, by then, it was night.

*

The next day I drove to have lunch with Aris's father, the novelist, who lived in the mountain village at the top of the island. I had been first introduced to him as "the novelist" and it's how I, and many others, still referred to him. We'd had a friendship prior to the one I'd had with Aris, from back when I was writing my dissertation. So it didn't strike me as particularly strange that he'd extend the invitation; it was hard to remain anonymous here. At the same time, driving up the winding mountain road, it felt as though I'd been summoned for a goodbye.

I left my car at the village's edge—you could not drive through the narrow passages, and because of this, the little streets into the village felt like corridors, the doors opening to rooms of one giant dwelling. You reach a sweet little overlook and quickly realize it's a private terrace.

The village felt clear and still, so different from the hectic ambiance near the port, from the beaches with their bars and tavernas. And after the bustle and noise and smells of Athens, it felt like another planet, with the island mountain stillness, the shock of bright flowers, the echoes from inside the dwellings nestled into the hills. It's a particular type of mountain repose, one I haven't felt anywhere else in the world.

I was early, so before turning the corner to the taverna I took a detour to wander the hushed, narrow streets. Colorful rugs hung from balconies, and I could hear the muted sounds of conversation, some violin music, the sound of silverware on plates.

I passed the novelist's house: his large red door and then the smaller green one of his guest studio, where I'd stayed many nights with Aris: a spaced detached from the main house, with its own entrance, bathroom, and tiny kitchenette. Though the two shared a wall, to reach it you had to exit the main home and walk ten steps down the narrow road. I had a flash of that younger self, the one in the gossip photo, stumbling back here with Aris, buzzed, after one of the famous dinners his father often hosted, headed to bed reeling from the joy of those hours just before dawn, fueled with wine and music and conversation. How we'd sometimes find the most stalwart of the guests having coffees the next morning, still at the table, not having slept. I'm romanticizing it a bit, I know, but I had really loved this life. It's when I felt my best, truest self.

The novelist and I sat down at Thanassis's, on its traditional terrace shaded with grape vines and shocks of pink flowers, at a table at the veranda's edge, looking over the valley. A huge plane tree stood grandly in the center. The actual kitchen was across the street—and by street I mean these narrow pedestrian walkways, no cars and only the occasional donkey, more like a corridor of a very large house—though there was a small bar within the café space itself. Sometimes Thanassis's son—Thanassis himself had died last year—plugged in an old, clunky television and set it atop the bar for soccer games.

When I was a graduate student, before Aris and I were together, I had spent two fascinating days listening to his father talk about the junta, which echoed the Nazi occupation, which echoed the Greek Civil War that started when the Germans left, and all of which was being echoed now. He kissed me hello and though this was not the first time I noticed it, Aris had his eyes—wide set, almond shaped, nearly black. My eyes, of course, were my mother's.

I lowered my gaze, and he leaned over the table and tipped my chin to him, the way my father used to do. "I'm so sorry,

Myrto," he said. It was the first time I'd seen him since my parents' funeral. I was used to this sort of sympathy, and though I was always glad for the kindness, I learned very quickly how to make people comfortable around my loss. But I realized he was also talking about Aris, and the freshness of the rejection surged through my body again, as if I were experiencing it for the first time.

I told him everything would be fine. I wanted to ask him if he'd known, but I couldn't bear to hear the answer, the humiliation of it. But as if reading my mind, he offered the information. "Aris only told me before he left for Brussels." I nodded again and let out a long, shaky exhale.

It seemed as though he wanted to say more. I feared that knot in my throat would become permanent, the tightness in my chest. "Of course we'll stay friends," he pronounced.

We shared a plate of lamb chops. Here in the mountain villages it was meat and meat and meat, which always surprised my father, who remembered an Athens childhood almost devoid of it. Everywhere you went it seemed people were grilling it. There was always an endless supply of local white wine in large plastic jugs. At first introduction I thought it would be terrible, but I've grown fond of it, the sharp barb of it that cuts the food, its soft back end.

The novelist topped off my glass again and again as the afternoon spiraled out, our conversation similarly circling and weaving, and I slowly relaxed. Aris had loved the way my mother would balk when he tried to pour her a drink, feigning shock if he poured too much, a gesture that would have been amusing had she not been slowly destroying her liver. Once, at a party to celebrate Aris's PhD defense, she gently tipped his bottle of beer so it would pour a bit more into her glass.

As for my mother, I have long ago replaced blame with sympathy for her behaviors that, as a teenager, I perceived to be inadequacies. Even in her moments of rage against me I'd understood that she did not mean them. In some ways I had distanced myself from my mother in the way I might view a grandparent: all-loving, a person you knew in a very specific capacity but you could not imagine their life before you, could not really know them. It was Aris who'd helped me with this, his push to give me an understanding of my parents through his Greek lens, through the lens of exile, through the lens of a difficult past. His own grandparents had been refugees, and he said that that trauma of forced migration was inherited. Eva promised him stability, tradition. I could give him many things, but not that.

There are no secrets. Everybody knows everything.

Everything is a lie, Kazantzidis sang.

The waiter cleared our plates, returned with a small platter of nectarines and berries.

"Myrto," the novelist said, hesitating over his first bite. "Have you seen Nefeli?"

I told him that since her show had opened, even before the vandalism, our visits had felt fragmented—Nefeli's moods had been more erratic than usual, and she often announced suddenly that she had to go or had another appointment, some changes to make at the museum or work to do at her studio. She was working on new paintings but forbade us to see them.

"I invited her for lunch last week," I said, "but she didn't respond."

"She's on the island," he said. So she had been here. Nefeli was a hard person to pin down, as if she moved quickly through portals.

"Listen," he said, after a pause. "I'm going to tell you something but you have to promise to pretend you do not know." I gestured for him to go on. He reached over and took my hands in his. "Nefeli is not well."

"Not well how?" I asked. He must have known about the stealing, the rapid changes in mood. I told him that without her pre-show adrenaline her mood had dimmed considerably.

"Around you she wants to pretend she's fine," he said.

I could feel that sharp twist in my guts again. It was true that Nefeli had grown distant, but I was used to the way we'd sometimes talk three times per day and other times she'd disappear for weeks into the labyrinthine space of her work, her mind. I knew she once had stayed with the novelist in the village, but in the past few years she'd converted an old shepherd's cottage into a small studio and now stayed there. Though I wouldn't be able to find it again, she'd brought me there once: it was charming and spartan and isolated, with a solar panel and rain barrel, a garden sprawling out back. "I want to die here," she'd said then, a disconcerting line that now felt alarming.

"She wants to imagine herself as a woman who is not sick. And that by doing so, she might become well." I recalled something the Captain had said: *From the moment I imagine something, it's a reality. It may only be in my mind, but a reality all the same.*

The novelist told me the details, though I sensed he knew even more than he was letting on. She'd been fighting a long time, trying all sorts of alternative treatments, including scorpion venom. I felt sick, thinking of the way a woman like Nefeli—independent, unconventional, rejecting tradition and societal norms—seemed forever due, at least here, in this country, to be punished.

Despite all the wine, I left the village soberer than I'd been in days.

*

The next morning I drove to my favorite beach, one you could only reach on foot from the road or by walking over the rocks and through the water from the adjacent cove. It was on the north end of the island, about fifteen kilometers from the mountain village. The road was so bumpy I thought the Fiat would just snap undone, all sides clattering to the ground.

I hiked down the familiar goat path and noticed something new at the end of the beach: a four-post bed in the small area of shade. The absurdity soothed me. Otherwise I was alone and was filled by the rush of this, no one knowing where I was.

I stripped down to my bikini bottoms, took a few steps into the water, and could feel myself opening up. What was the source of this near-spiritual ecstasy? The sense of being on the border of earth and sea? Or something primordial, the way fish crawled out of the ocean to live on land, the way we might wish for gills or almost feel the sprouting of wings from our shoulder blades?

The water was freezing, and I wasn't quite ready for it, so I lay down atop the blanket. The sun was warm on my back. I fell into a heavy nap and dreamt of Nefeli, waking unsettled. I sent her a text but I had no service and it didn't go through.

After noon, the day grew warm. From my bag I retrieved the apricots and cherries I'd purchased from the vendor at the side of the road, the cheese pie. I drank half the bottle of water and flipped to my front. I drifted in and out of sleep, and when I stood up I noticed an older woman on the bed, dressed in a black housedress, also asleep, her body curled up beneath a blanket, her back to me. I hadn't heard or seen her arrive. When I walked closer I could hear her snoring.

I swam and swam, back and forth, back and forth, a quick, measured freestyle going nowhere, between the two capes that enclosed the cove. Then I decided to swim farther, to see how far I could go, to see if I could reach the rock out in the distance. In high school I had been a swimmer, and it felt good to channel all the power of my body into measured, strong strokes: *one two three four five breathe, one two three four five breathe.*

I grew tired soon enough, wondering what had gotten into me. Finally, I flipped onto my back and whipped my goggles off my face, letting them dangle in my hand. I floated, trying not to move, and let the salty sea gently prop me up. *No one knows where I am.* I looked up and could still, though barely, see the bed on the shore, smaller now in the distance, rising and falling with the gentle undulations of the waves. I had the strange feeling of seeing my strokes from above, as if I were both myself and some woman I was watching from the separate point of that bed, ashore.

I was much farther out than I had realized. I was so far into the sea that I was a part of it. Up above, a helicopter hovered. Not far from me was a yacht, though probably not as close as it seemed. I lay still atop the waves awhile. When I became cold I replaced my goggles, making sure they were tight and sealed, and began the swim back, which took all the strength I had, my small lunch long ago burned off. *One two three four five. Breathe.* The rhythm of my strokes, the fullness in my lungs, all those jumbled fragments racing through my mind. Last summer. My mother and the scorpion fish. Her failing liver. The doctor's alarm: *The sting is very dangerous. Particularly in her state. We must be very careful. We will keep her for a few days.*

What state, I asked the doctor. *What state,* I asked my father. *It's her liver,* the doctor told me. *Her liver can't process it. How much does she drink a day.* My father's defensiveness. *She doesn't drink more than anybody else. How much.*

How much?

I'm getting married, Aris said.

One two three four five. Breathe breathe. Breathe.

She's having a baby, he said.

Nefeli's not well, the novelist said.

I began to swim as though I had just shot off the block in a race, my sixteen-year-old body emerging from within me, lean and strong and trained and understanding how to use the water, to work with it, not against it. The pounding of my heart propelled me forward, a hot little engine. I sliced the water with my hands with a rage that seemed to have no end. My mother on the dread of another Chicago winter: *It will kill me, Myroula. Your father won't leave. He wants to stay here forever. Until we die.*

I'm getting married. I'm going to be a father.

She wants to imagine herself as a woman who is not sick.

I was certain I heard music but that was impossible, some sort of minor-keyed singing, but still I slowed my pace to trace it, to listen more closely. It vanished. I began to kick harder and the voices came back. This was not the place to unravel. I kept this pace until finally the seafloor looked as though I could touch it, so many sea urchins. If I was careful I could avoid them. *A scorpion fish. The sting is venomous. Her health is not good. How could you not have realized this?*

I felt something touch my ankle and I lurched up, flinging off my goggles and flipping my hair out of my face. I flung myself onto my back, tried to keep my mouth above the waterline, tasted salt, spit. My lungs burning.

I finally dragged myself out of the water, slouched over, exhausted, a waterlogged shell of the woman I was. A young couple stood on the shore with their hands on their hips, watching me slog through the water. The man called out to ask if I was okay. I couldn't speak but I nodded, waved my goggles in the air, to answer them. I felt exposed and naked and was glad my wet hair hung over my breasts. What did the others see? An exhausted, topless figure coming out of the water like some drunken, graceless sea nymph? The inverse of a fully clothed woman walking into the sea with stones in her pockets to drown herself?

When I reached the shore, the woman approached me with a large thick towel and wrapped it around my shoulders. The gesture was so tender I felt a knot form in my throat. My legs buckled. I was shivering.

The yiayia who'd been sleeping on the bed trudged over, pointing up at the helicopter and saying that I was lucky the coast guard was watching. What was I doing swimming so far, and didn't I know there were dangerous currents? She waved her hand in the air and then crossed herself. As if she had commanded it, the helicopter rose up and away, back toward some other place in the sky.

The old woman studied my face, my towel-wrapped body, my feet, then looked straight into my eyes. "*Tinos eisai?*" she asked. It was a phrase I had not heard since I was a child, from my grandparents. She pushed a lock of hair off of my face. *Whose are you?* She was asking. *To whom do you belong?*

Silence can be terrifying, and the longer I was quiet, the more rattled she became. She asked if I was foreign. I couldn't form words. The younger woman tried to help: "Italian? Bulgarian? Arabic?" Something in my eyes must have alarmed the older one, because she exclaimed, "Girl! Do we need to call a doctor?"

Did we? The angle of the setting sun felt noisy, her voice was painful on my shivering skin, and the smell of the younger woman's body lotion stung my eyes. My senses fired and merged and failed, everything jumbled up.

I finally spoke, in Greek, and assured everyone I was okay. I did not want them to see the way I was trembling. I did not want them to think I was mad. I sat down on my blanket and the old woman watched me, her hands on her hips. Across the small beach my mother stood by the bed, pressing down on the mattress. She sat down and lay back, as if embarrassed by my antics. Too much attention.

With the towel still around me I removed my swimsuit and pulled on my underwear. I handed her back her towel and pulled on my T-shirt. Then she hugged me, as if we were sisters in our bedroom and I had told her something horrible. Me in my white cotton underwear, she in her boyfriend's shirt. She said she'd thought she'd seen two women out there—had I gone in alone?

I told her I had, which seemed to distress her. Her boyfriend watched, patiently, as if he had witnessed something he wasn't supposed to but had no other choice. Then he came over to say goodbye. What sort of wretchedness they saw in me I didn't want to consider. My hair was already beginning to dry in crazy, salty waves; a waterlogged Medusa in underwear, heavy indents from the goggles on my face.

When they left, I changed into a pair of jeans—an old, soft pair, warm from the sun, and a sweatshirt. My skin was covered with goose bumps, and the touch of the soft fabric on my skin was so good I could have cried. Though the air was warm, I was deeply chilled, shivering from primal place. I curled up on the blanket and let the air rush from my lungs. Below my heavy, closed eyelids I could feel my pulse, keeping time.

The beach was silent now, the sea quiet, and I lay still, not wanting to disturb any of it, not wanting to turn it to stone.

I gathered my things as the last light faded from the sky. I was light-headed with hunger. I could go to one of the tavernas with the gorgeous views, but the thought of eating alone suddenly felt unbearable. I'd get something at the port. To hold me over I stopped instead at a little bakery, about to close, and bought some sesame cookies and orange juice, like I'd just given blood. Then I got into my car and ate three of the cookies, crumbs falling all over my jeans, the seat. I drank the container of juice all at once, some of it dribbling on my chin, which I wiped with my sleeve. I drove away.

*

Although my parents had died in Chicago, an accident in the snow, in my mind it's always here, on this stretch of road. I don't know why. The day they died my father had been driving, though probably because my mother was drunk. He hated driving, and my desire to learn at sixteen baffled him. But once I'd learned, he loved when I'd drive him around. When we'd attend gatherings together he'd tell his friends I had driven, as though he were telling him I'd taken them there in my helicopter, or flown in on a magic carpet.

I was grateful for the dark drive, the ability to only see ten feet ahead. No more than I needed, a need-to-know basis. Still, I kept my eyes sharp for a woman walking as if she'd come from the sea. The darkness was a relief. I didn't want to be reminded of that spectacular landscape, the twists and turns and gorgeous sea views. At that moment I needed the anonymity of night driving, the near terror of turning a sharp, steep corner and feeling I might fly off the cliff. I needed to feel the dropping heft inside me as I veered straight into the black night sky, only my headlights to remind me of the surrounding darkness.

Wasn't facing loss the same? *Breathe in, breathe out.* To see the entire landscape was just too much, the green hills in the distance, the setting sun over the glass sea, the vibrant supermoon. Grief was oceanic; you could get lost in it, as if swimming in deep water while not knowing which end was up. For a moment I experienced the intense sensation of someone next to me, but the passenger seat held only my bag. I thought of the professional mourners, those women hired to lament at funerals, to perform grief, and I finally understood the point. Grief never appeared the way we expected, and it snuck up in terrifying, surprising waves.

Others needed to see it translated into something visceral and simple, something that could be read, understood. Because when we're in its midst it cannot be translated at all.

In the small rooftop shed, I found the furniture I had dragged up there a few summers ago, my father protesting that I'd hurt myself hauling it up there but then being delighted by the rooftop sitting area. I pulled out one of the two divans and a small wooden table. Years ago, Aris and I had slept up there, beneath thin cotton blankets and the bright night sky. I woke in the middle of the night, and he was standing at the ledge, looking out at the view; from there you could see the dark sea. And then I realized he was pissing out onto the narrow alley. I didn't want to startle him so I just watched, amusedly, and when he turned to come back to bed he saw me sitting up and he shrugged, laughed.

I poured the last two shots from a bottle of whiskey into a glass, took a sip, and set it aside. Before I could change my mind, I emptied out my parents' closets and drawers—there were not many things—into a separate bag, saving a soft oxford and a gray T-shirt of my father's, and an elegant trench coat and two silk scarves of my mother's, all of which she'd had since before my birth. I pulled my wild beach hair back in a scarf and put the oxford on over my hot skin. I tried on the jacket, slipped on my mother's slippers. In every hiding space, the chest of blankets and sweaters, the linen closet, the bathroom cabinet, there were near-empty liquor bottles. I gathered them into a bag.

Now, the whiskey burned and I enjoyed it. Drink still in hand, I walked back to the dumpster. First I tossed the empty bottles, again satisfied to hear the crash of more glass breaking. Then I was about to toss in the old clothes but instead left them in the shopping bag, on the ground. Perhaps someone would find them. I knew I was about to face another salty wave of grief, and at least I knew what to expect. Its familiarity soothed me. It belonged to me, just the way that living in two worlds, two lives, was my way of being. I approached each return as I did the seasons, the change of weather leaving me momentarily bewildered as to what to wear. Each time I arrived in Greece it was as if I had rediscovered it again. Who would I now be in this place? I had never answered the old woman: *To whom do you belong?*

Two young backpackers walked by, looking lost, but the sight of me hurling things into a dumpster, dressed like a lunatic and holding a glass of whiskey, probably didn't make me seem a person to ask for directions. They hurried past me, in the shamed way we deal with the insane—the man murmuring to himself on the bus, the crazy lady in the central square feeding the pigeons.

Of course I couldn't *not* think of Aris, the way we'd emptied the entire brownstone that way, in a frenzy. Garbage bag by garbage bag: underwear drawers, socks, papers, and old bills that perhaps should have been kept, but I heaved those into the dumpster, too.

It may seem that because I took Aris's news with such nonchalance that I was not hurt by it. I was. But I don't construct a narrative of myself as a loyal, faithful girlfriend, unraveled by Aris's sexual infidelity. It was more complicated than that: our relationship had never been conventional. It was that he'd moved on, completely present in this new life with Eva, and we had not even had a proper breakup, a proper goodbye. We never assumed sexual fidelity but we, at least I, assumed some sort of loyalty. Maybe I was naïve to actually think there was a difference. What

I had taken for devotion was simply complacency, the most dangerous state of all.

No, I wasn't naïve. But I wasn't *not* naïve either. I could say this about almost anything, my life of betweenness. I was not reeling. A pregnancy, a life with someone who was not me, one that had begun months before I knew. This is what doubled me over. Aris had been living two parallel lives and now they had met. I, too, had been living two lives: my life in the States and my life here, but somehow my rootlessness had become its own sort of trap.

Back in the house, I felt relieved by the absence of things that did not belong to me. Two of Nefeli's paintings hung over the couch, several long-faced women seated around a table. I called her yet again but she didn't pick up.

No, I was still reeling. Had I not still been reeling from the breakup I would have understood Nefeli's behavior to be direr than I had. That her odd behavior was not artistic tempestuousness but something more bruised, desperate. Even self-destructive.

The couple on the beach had thought they'd seen *two* women out there swimming, and I wondered who had been out there with me and what had happened to her. Maybe I was both in the water and on land, all at once. Maybe I had somehow finally really split myself in two: the woman I was then and the woman I was becoming, both of us out there carving through the waves. I sipped my drink and wondered how long it would be before my mother emerged from inside me, how long I could keep her hidden deep inside before she broke through my skin, triumphant.

16

Mira

That evening, after my afternoon at the sea, I was anxious, buzzing, unable to sit still. I tidied up, went through a few things, found a few books I'd wanted to read. Kyria Voula, whom I had not yet seen but seemed to appear when I wasn't around, had left a bowl of strawberries on the table, and a small ceramic pot of homemade yogurt in the fridge, which I ate. She'd taken down my laundry and folded it on my bed. I texted Dimitra to call me, then went out for a walk.

The port was crowded. At the far end, passengers boarded the ferry. I ate a souvlaki on a bench, looking out at the small sailboats, the fishing vessels, the larger, more elegant crafts whose owners either stood in front, proud and admiring, or were nowhere to be found. I was gripped by loneliness.

Of course Nefeli was ill. How had I not known, or, more accurately, how could I not have admitted it to myself? I'd attributed it all to depression alone, as if the mind were not part of the body. The stealing, the small rages, the gray pallor and the darkness below her eyes. From that very first outing to the beach when I'd arrived: it was all there, in plain sight.

From the distance I could hear music. Singing, a coo of voices, minor keys: humming? Low registers and high ones, intense harmonies that intensified and retreated, growing quiet for a moment. At first I thought it was coming from one of the docked sailboats, some beautiful and eerie nautical choir. I looked around to see if anyone else heard it; it was so subtle I thought I was going mad. One second it would sound like praise and the other like lament, from keening to joy, taunting me like impish angels.

I glanced around, wished I could share the moment with someone, if for no other reason than to confirm it. People walked by in twos and threes, couples holding hands, families, groups of loud teenagers. Nobody seemed to hear it.

That's when I noticed him, the Captain. His face was brown with sun, his shirt was pressed, his hair seemed longer, messy, and he hadn't shaved in probably a few days. I almost didn't recognize him, but the entire effect was quite lovely. I so rarely looked at his face. Only a glimpse here and there: over the balcony, a sun-drenched moment on the roof, a walk from the market on the street behind our building.

"Mira," he said. "Mira away from Athens." He took a seat on the far end of the bench.

"Please tell me you hear that," I said. I could feel his glance. I raised my hand over my eyes to turn toward him in the flush of sunset. The sound, like a rush of urgent, human voices. For the longest time he was quiet and I wondered if I had spoken or just thought I had spoken.

"It's the wind moving through the sails." He said a few other boat terms I didn't understand, which he repeated in English, as though that might help: the rigging and the halyards. For some reason sea sickness hadn't come to me until I was a teenager, despite the fact that children are more susceptible to it, but without question, for me to get on a sailboat is to spend it sick and leaning over the edge, just like my mother, forever wondering why I'd thought that particular time might be different.

"The sails?" I asked.

"Yes. Call them the sails."

I couldn't explain the knot in my throat. I was afraid if I didn't concentrate on it hard enough it would fade. "I could listen to this all night," I said. I felt embarrassed and hoped all the emotion didn't show in my face. But who was I kidding. I was transparent. All that from wind—like sirens, like sea nymphs.

We listened. He glanced over his shoulder. Maybe he was waiting for his family. A few times I could see he went to speak but something stopped him, like a wall drawing down, blocking the words. It was the strangest feeling. I was going to ask him if he was okay, something I might do on the balcony, but here it felt too intimate. For a brief moment our hands touched, but neither of us pulled away. He folded his hand over mine.

After a few minutes, he removed his hand, stood, and turned away as casually as he would have stepped back through the door of his apartment, and continued walking down the promenade. I walked in the other direction along the port, past the ferries and up the hill. I stopped at the small, scraggly beach at the end of town, where a young woman kicked a soccer ball around with her dog. There was a small fishing boat, moored in the sand, half in sea, half on land, its bottom flat and sinking as if it might belong there, might be best suited to that position.

I don't know why I felt so moved. I wished he'd sat with me longer, or that we'd taken a walk, there but at the time I couldn't find any words. As odd as it sounds, it was the first time we'd conversed in public. Perhaps I was afraid to disrupt that speculative space we had created for ourselves, my contingent freedom from my body. We had been constructing a fiction that had nothing to do with our individual realities. Yet something was happening there. An emergence.

17

Mira

When the novelist called three days later to tell me that Nefeli had shown up at his house and was now staying in the guest room, the implication of his call was clear. I wanted to see her but because I knew something I was not supposed to know, I hesitated. That Nefeli *wanted* me to pretend I knew nothing made the deception trickier and obligatory and multilayered and exhausting. Her behavior was intense self-preservation: perform it, believe it, make it so.

When I arrived in the village, Nefeli was in the small daybed, reading. I didn't ask why she wasn't staying in her cottage on the hill, though had I not known she was sick I would have. Or why she wasn't staying in the private guest studio, where I usually stayed, but in the large back room of the main house that the novelist usually used as a study. The entire room was sparsely furnished in a way that made it feel even larger than it was. Now the space had been taken over by paintings, lining the entire perimeter of the room, backs facing out to hide their subjects. I could smell the reek of acrylic and thinner.

She looked up, irritated, as if she'd been expecting me and I was late. I asked her how she was, and she said she was fine. She got out of bed and shuffled to the straight-backed chair next to the window. Beside it was a desk draped in a white sheet, covered with brushes and tubes of oil paint, small glass jars of what I assumed was solvent, sketch pads and pencils and drawing paper.

I was in a loose sundress and sweating from the walk up into the village, but she was in flannel pajamas. I was supposed to pretend all this was normal for her at three in the afternoon, to be crippled by pain, to have her face permanently cringed. To not have responded to any of our messages. When I'd seen her last, after all, listening to the cicadas, it had felt like a goodbye.

Now she was here in front of me but something felt off, as if this woman were only a shadow of Nefeli, a projection, an image beamed in from somewhere else. I touched her shoulder gently, and she eyed me strangely.

"I ran out of space up there," she said, waving first in the direction of her cottage and then to the paintings. She walked to the nightstand, poured herself a glass of water from a pitcher and drank it in one motion. "Do you want something to drink?" she asked, gasping.

I felt as though I were choking. "Everyone's been worried."

"Let them dye their hair pink, orange, green," Nefeli said, "if they want to express themselves. Let them stand outside the metro with a megaphone and take a selfie. Look at them all, with their tattoos and piercings and strange clothing. Who cares."

I had been talking about me and Fady and Dimitra, but I lowered my voice, as if coaxing a cat from a tree. "Those young artists," I said. "They admire you. They don't want you to be silenced."

The softer my voice, the more infuriated Nefeli's became. "They have no idea what that means. To be silenced. They talk so much they have no idea what they mean."

Nefeli seemed to be waiting for me to leave, which I did. I stepped outside, if only because I had no idea what to do with my body. I heard the gurgle of her water pipe, smelled the sweet smoke through the open window.

I found the novelist coming down the hill, his legs a bit bow-legged; I realized he walked just like Aris. I'm surprised I hadn't noticed it before.

"I've never seen her this agitated," I said, quietly. We moved away from the door.

"She refuses to talk to me," he said. "Yet she wants to stay in the house. Aliki brings her food and juice, says she's often in conversation with someone not in the room. This morning Aliki helped her wash her hair, but Nefeli refused help drying it. It's as if she doesn't even hear me."

He told me she was staying up all night, drawing or painting. "I suspect she's in unimaginable pain," he said. Often during the days she disappeared to her cottage. Nikos drove her. She was too frail to take those narrow, uneven stone stairs herself, and he drove his pickup truck all the way to the door.

Then, suddenly, the front door of the novelist's house flung open. There stood Nefeli, framed by the arch. She was still in her pajamas, plus a drover hat and leather jacket.

I felt as though I had been discovered with a lover by a jealous spouse. Her expression was pure disgust, but there was something frightened, dejected in her face.

I'd betrayed her, somehow. By going along with the façade that we both knew I was going along with? I had thought that was the way she wanted it, despite my discomfort. I now think she wanted me to challenge her, all this time, to force myself to face it. She had been broken by Haroula, a woman who could never quite acknowledge their love, could never be as public as Nefeli would have liked. What is a relationship in secret? She wanted to know. It's not real. It's nothing more than a dream.

I don't know if I agreed, but I had spent a lot of time thinking of it.

Had she thought we—I and the novelist and the Captain and Fady and Dimitra—were not talking about her? That I was performing obliviousness not only for Nefeli but also for the novelist and everyone else I encountered? That in our dealings I had also convinced myself she was fine?

"I don't want you to write about any of this," she said. "Nothing. Not my art, not my love affairs. Definitely not my politics." Then she waved her hand over her body, as if to say, *Especially not this.*

"And you," she said. "Even when I vanish."

"Please don't vanish," I said.

"We deal with all of it and shield the men from its effects. Let them deal with the shit they create. You stupid girl. It's all shit."

She was rambling, she was all over the place, as if time wound around her in spirals, saying one thing and then unraveling it the next moment. "Both of you: write this down. Why aren't you writing this down? Your little books, your little stories."

"Your *oral histories*," she said to me. "Your little *projects*. Bah."

"And you. Your stupid novels," she said to him. "I dare you. Write it."

She turned back inside and we followed. She asked for some hot water and lemon. "I'm detoxifying my body," she said with a cackle. But when I brought it to her in her room, she became exasperated.

The novelist asked me to stay the night, and I knew it was because he thought Nefeli might need me. We sat on his balcony, which was narrow and long and overlooked the valley. From there the world felt nearly still, nearly calm, nearly sane. Nefeli slept, and though she was at the other end of the house we kept our voices low. I asked him about the scorpions, which Nefeli's new paintings seemed obsessed with. Her new drawings had the faces of haggard women on the bodies of scorpions, or thin, young women with grasping claws for hands, and segmented tails. It's gruesome looking, the most gruesome I've seen her work be.

He told me the only other place in the world he could imagine himself living—that he'd visited, at least—was Cuba. Maybe Spain. Landscapewise, culture, he said.

He often talked in what seemed like non sequiturs; his novels were the same way. So I waited. It was as if no story had a true beginning, so you could always take it back and back.

He had gone there with Nefeli, he said, to Havana, on first diagnosis, when she became obsessed with scorpion venom. It was before things were readily available on the internet, or, at least, available to them. "You had to go to Cuba. Nefeli insisted.

So we went to get it and brought it back. It worked, for a while, or seemed to." Now, she had found an easier way to get it but he didn't think it was working.

"You went together?" I asked.

"Yes," he said. "The two of us. She needed someone with her," he said. "Aris didn't know," he added.

"You have a special friendship," I said.

"Don't let that fool you. There's nothing like the bond of marriage. Larger than life."

I had certainly heard such words before, but their sincerity, from him, shocked me. Do we all become more sentimental in our old age, or wiser? "I hope you will marry," he said. "I'm sorry it's not Aris. I wanted *you* as my daughter-in-law." Whether he truly believed it, it moved me that he had said it. "When you're young you think it's all you want, and then you find it simply silly. As you get older you see what it means." I wondered if he'd said these things to Aris before, about me.

It may seem ridiculous now, considering my age, but it's been only in the last few years that I've understood that independence and love need not be mutually exclusive, that we don't have to give up one to have the other. Fady and Dimitra, both independent, both continuing to grow, to do their work, to make friends, yet something so solid between them. My parents had given me a controlling, smothering, nearly aggressive love, and I had never allowed myself, not with Aris and not with any man before him, to give myself to a relationship. How could it be that it took me until I had nearly turned forty to begin to know something of love, that I'd spent the greater part of my life living inside the rigid boundaries I'd crafted for myself?

I had not realized what I had been missing. The beauty of growing up with a person. I had had that with Aris, in a way. Sometimes we'd lived together, other times apart; sometimes we broke up and would see other people, but then I'd come back to Greece or he'd come to the States and all would be forgiven. Yet in my mind I always imagined we'd end up together. Whatever that means. He was for me a representation not only of love but of Greece, of the place my parents and I had left behind, and as such I had somehow thought we were beyond the more common stresses of a relationship. We had become proficient at long distance and I mistook this for our relationship's strength. He was always waiting for the relationship to begin, whereas I'd thought what we had *was* the relationship. Maybe I'd given him strength to move on. A solid foundation from which to leap.

I didn't drive back to the port that night, opting to stay in the guest house. As I crept through the gate, down the stairs, I couldn't help but peek in Nefeli's window, which was wide open, the light on. But she wasn't there. The bed wasn't made, a tangle of sheets. I glanced around the courtyard, expecting her to come up behind me.

When I got back to the guest house, I went to the small bottom drawer of the bureau, the one where I always left my things. A few T-shirts, underwear, a few notebooks and a plastic baggie full of makeup and pens. For a moment, I hesitated. Like Shrödinger's cat, they were both there and not there until the moment I opened the drawer. I tried to remember the firsts: the first time I'd slept here, the first time I came to think of this space as my own, the first time I learned Nefeli was sick. I could barely recall a moment. I could barely recall chronology. I could barely recall what was mine.

I've always slept soundly on the island, but Nefeli's earlier scorn had unhinged me, as had being back in this place without Aris. I drifted in and out of awakenings, strange dreams, and paralyzed wakefulness. Finally, I was overcome with the desire to be outside.

Three o'clock in the morning, midweek, and the village was quiet, so quiet I felt exposed, half expecting faces to emerge from the shadows, or figures to hold lanterns to my face. I focused on objects: doorknobs, the shadowy center of a tree trunk, an alcove, or plant beneath a door.

Strolling through those narrow streets at this hour, I experienced the same eerie sensation I'd felt sleepwalking through my own house as a child, unable to recognize it. I had to ask myself a few times if I was indeed asleep.

When I reached Thanassis's, I relaxed at the familiarity, though now that it was closed, empty, the huge plane tree seemed different, the restaurant spacious, cavernous. I walked right up the three steps and sat at a table, as if expecting to be served.

My mother sat at the bar with my father and several other friends, and Thanassis was behind it. A carafe of raki in front of them, a haze of cigarette smoke. I didn't recognize all of them. One of them was Traianos, a friend I'd loved, who died the night of my thirtieth birthday, in a horrible, senseless accident. A woman with long, straight black hair, her back to me, swayed her hips, and when she turned for a moment it looked like Nefeli, but it was not. There was no sadness in their faces. They were laughing, singing, drinking. For a brief second my mother caught my eye and she smiled—something warm and conspiratorial—but then she turned back to her friends. Somehow I understood this might be her last drink.

The chairs had been placed on the tables. I sat down at my usual space, in the corner, where the seats lined the walls, a long booth along the side of the restaurant, facing the open canyon. I took one chair down and propped my feet atop it. From there I could see the tiny cemetery lit up, the lights from other villages, all the way down to the lights that lit the port, still bustling and alive at this hour. I felt sleepy, my body suddenly heavy. I wasn't ready to go back to bed but I felt as though I could sleep right there.

The moonlight drenched the taverna like a torrent of rain would. The village was so still I felt hypervisible, as if I were walking through a deserted terrain of one of Rami's video games. I took a photo of the landscape in front of me: a physical correspondence to remember this numbness. The lights from a few clusters of houses lit up the side of the mountain. If I leaned over the edge of the half wall—up to my chest—I'd fall down into the ravine, into the valley. I felt safe there, though, on this side of the void.

Then I felt a strange surge of joy despite the circumstances, and, for the first time in my life, inexplicably free.

That's when I glanced to the entrance and saw a tall figure there, glowing in the moonlight. I jumped, felt a strange pull behind my belly button, a tingle near the top of my spine. Half fear, half arousal. A man. A light-gray T-shirt and matching sweatpants, like a track star from 1985. Gray running shoes whose bottoms lit up like fireflies. The glint of his glasses. A familiar, pleasant feeling.

The Captain. He looked to the bar then back to me. I wondered what *he* saw there, what tableau of loss.

"I didn't mean to frighten you," he said. He spoke in Greek. "You startled *me*, in fact."

He shifted on his feet, as if ready to break into a run. I became aware that he'd been in my thoughts. I felt a wash of relief— someone else, alive and walking around at this hour. Let alone *this* someone else.

"I was walking and saw you."

You as in *me*? Or you as in a person. I still couldn't tell if he recognized me. I realized I had not yet spoken and that my silence was probably unsettling. "Do you want to join me?" My voice sounded different: thick and deep. I gestured around the taverna to the seat in front of me, as if it were the middle of the afternoon. For a moment he didn't move. Didn't laugh, or even smile. Was he sleepwalking? My mother used to sleepwalk and it always frightened me: she would suddenly be standing in my doorway, laughing, and say something crazy, like, *Oh, you! You're a paper finger! You've come for the furniture train, wait for the celery, do you need an umbrella or a bookcase?*

I was hesitant. You're not supposed to wake a sleepwalker. Why? Heart attack? But then he sidled over, as if we were in a crowded bar and had met eyes across the room.

"It would be nice to have something to drink," he said.

Neither of us said anything for a moment. It was not awkwardness.

"Insomnia?" I asked.

He nodded. "A dangerous place to sleepwalk," he said, looking past me, over the cliff.

He walked across the dark restaurant to behind the now-empty bar, and then he disappeared into the kitchen, which apparently was not even locked. He came back with a beer and two small tumblers. "Don't worry," he said. "The owner is a friend. I've been coming here since I was a child."

I slid my feet off the chair but he sat down next to me—not too close—on the bench, but there was something both pal-ish and warm about the gesture. He leaned back and crossed his ankle over his knee. He wore white ankle running socks with a blue stripe at the top. Endearing. His physicality, the everydayness of it. He offered me a cigarette.

"Oh why not." He lit it for me. "Always quitting."

"I remember."

"Your father?" I asked, after a moment.

"He's fine. Holed up on the hill, in Nefeli's cottage this whole time. Obsessed with his bees. Something both selfless and self-centered. Careful tending, with no response, no acknowledgment. Honey. In his old age, this sort of careful, repetitive task, wrapped up in solitude, suits him."

"Okay," he added. "The truth is, he's losing his mind."

"I'm sorry," I said.

He sighed and looked as though he were ready to divulge some painful secret. We had not been in the habit of talking these last weeks; we had forgotten our rhythms, and anyway, we were not used to the other's physical presence.

I tried to store his face in my memory then. His hair was graying slightly at the temples and otherwise was nearly blond from the sun. High cheekbones. Behind his glasses, eyes like a big cat. His nose was sunburned; I could tell by the light of the moon.

Otherwise, there was a heaviness to the space, a density to his presence, our joint presence here that was somehow pitched at an angle to everything else.

The rest of the world was quiet, and the Captain began to speak.

"So I'd been right. Katerina is in love. She swears nothing has happened, that she did not cheat. Anyway, I hate that word, *cheat*, to act dishonorably to obtain something advantageous. The word alone makes a mockery of marriage. Besides, how can she help the way she feels? I'm not telling you about my moments of jealousy, irrational rage, or the circular conversations I've put her through, exhausting us both. I suppose at times I was furious but I knew I had no right to be.

"Everything I do in life feels like an atonement for earlier behavior. My last day on the ship, when we arrived at Piraeus, my quartermaster informed me that our supervisor was waiting for me. He'd come in from the company's headquarters in Brussels. I knew he was there for other business as well, but I also knew that the main point was to see me. I packed my bags, took down the notecards and photos and things I would miss. I knew that I would not sleep in that small cabin again. The walk to his office was a long one.

"'*We know you were acting out of kindness, not of malice,*' he said.

"Of course it was kindness. It was beyond kindness. It was duty. Collusion with smugglers, they said. That would assume I'd been rewarded, and I had not. Someone I trusted had come to me, asked for help. It was humanitarian, I thought. Not criminal. Facilitating migration was the charge. Well, yes. Isn't that also what a ship captain does? Language, here, will distort, and when you take something too literally it nearly disappears. But it's true I had looked the other way. It had seemed like the right thing to do.

"Anyway. For me, nothing feels more dispiriting than the idea of staying in one place, yet for some I know it's a luxury. And each year I veer closer to that very thing—from the long voyages in the Pacific to those shorter European routes. Maybe next, if I am lucky, I'll have some shorter Aegean routes or even something ashore, my old life disappearing like the green flash of the sun as it dips below the horizon—until I'll go no farther than the kiosk for my newspapers and cigarettes, like my father, whose furthest movement from the home, until recently, was an occasional drive to the next town for coffee or afternoons down at the beach for a swim. Mostly he moves between the house, the café, and his bees, which he began keeping after politics had worn him down. The body holds memory longer than the mind."

"It's no wonder I remain in limbo."

At what point did I shift in my seat, sit cross-legged, and touch his arm? At what point did I stand to refill our water glasses? At what point did we finish the beer and get another? The details of the chronology are hazy but the events are clear, hyperfocused. When I returned with a full carafe of water the Captain pulled me onto his lap, facing him, and my hands fell naturally around his neck, played with that fine hair there, then moved down over his shoulders. He let out a long breath, something beside a sigh and a groan. He moved his hands under my shirt. "Is this okay," he asked.

I remember the early purpley light, and the sunrise, which came way too soon.

18

The Captain

I returned to my father's home at dawn, and when I woke a few hours later I replayed the night with Mira in my mind. When I went into the kitchen, my father was having his breakfast on the terrace that overlooked the valley. I poured myself a cup of coffee, adding a lot of milk and sugar, and stood at the counter, trying to delineate where the night had ended. I brought the coffee pot outside and refilled my father's cup. He thanked me absentmindedly, like I did this every day, and stirred in his sugar. The church bells chimed, but otherwise the village was quiet.

My father was always meticulous about his breakfast: a loaf of bread on a wooden tray, a cloth napkin draped over it, a serrated knife to cut it. A little pot of butter, a little pot of jam. Fruit. Brewed coffee; Greek coffee was for the afternoon. He usually read the papers but they sat stacked on the table, untouched. He saw me eye them and shrugged.

When I sat he passed me the bread and asked me again about Katerina. Was he being polite or did he know something more? I wondered what Katerina had told him. Had he heard me leave in the middle of the night, then return at sunrise? Not interrupting, not saying a thing, my father listened to me talk for some time.

"There are no secrets," he said to me, and I could tell he also knew I was no longer working. But his tone was not accusatory, as I would have guessed. Just matter-of-fact. It was early but the sun beat down, and I had to keeping wiping my brow with a napkin. My father, though, appeared unbothered by it. In fact, he seemed overall quite well that morning, not forgetting words or mixing things up, or acting as though the very distant past was right behind us in the kitchen. I knew this didn't mean much—I guessed he was always best in the morning—but it calmed me a bit.

My father cut up a nectarine and handed me a slice. He would never say something like, *Whatever makes you happy*. It's not the way he saw the world. Happiness, to him, was a by-product, not a goal, an idea I was beginning to share.

After breakfast, I drove to the closest beach for a swim.

It was the less-traveled side of the island, away from the port. But the road to the water had recently been widened and cleared, and now crawled with rental jeeps and foreign plates and a mini-mart, a few rickety beach bars. I could hear the whoops and cries of tourists posing for photos, men flexing their muscles and looking dumbly at the camera, women with that empty, stupid-faced stare that at some point so many not-stupid women took on as customary.

I turned around and drove to the more secluded, lesser-known cove nearby. At the far end a couple slept, faces down, their bodies splayed out like starfish. I took a quick dip to cool off, then read for a while, a book of short stories organized around the stops of the Athens train, my breathing slowing to that pleasant, slow reading rhythm. Every so often an image from the night before: a shift of the body, a look on Mira's face, her bare shoulder, would come into my mind, and I would stop reading for a moment. And I had told her so many things, things I could barely admit to myself.

Then I took a long swim. When we were at the beach, I always splashed around with the kids, playing games, but I can't remember the last time I swam out with no purpose. I missed the sea deeply: being on it, being in it. Then I stopped moving and floated on my back awhile. Though I can't say I hadn't enjoyed this period of idleness—I had, very much—I was too young to retire. I wasn't ready. I allowed myself, for the first time, to wish for something: it was my own hesitation that kept me from even acknowledging a need. My marriage had long ago become unsalvageable, perhaps, but maybe my job was still within reach. I would call my boss again this afternoon. If not that job, another one.

When I emerged from the water an hour later, the starfish couple was packing up their things. The woman had long black hair and wore a black striped bikini and a crocheted cover-up that reminded me of a doily. She looked nice. The man wore a bathing suit printed with octopuses. I watched them wind back up the path in their flip-flops, heard their car start and drive away.

I remained on my small towel. The sea had turned a deep blue-black, and the sun was hidden behind some menacing clouds, low and dark. I could feel pressure on my temples, behind my eyes, along with a general uneasiness, a subterranean dread. I drank the rest of my water and began the steep hike back to the car.

For some reason I took a slightly different path up. I stopped to take a piss and suddenly was hit with a wretched smell. Something organic, rotting.

I looked up ahead and in the thicket I saw a dead goat, as if it had slipped and fallen. There were many wild goats on the island, so many that sometimes they stopped traffic. Other times they managed to hike down to the steep cliffs over the water, near the monastery, and couldn't find their way back up. You might see them from a boat and wonder how they ever made it there in the first place. Often they died there. But after the fires earlier this year, on this end of the island, nothing would grow back with the goats roaming around, so people were encouraged to shoot them. The logical solution of a crazy person. I didn't love the idea of armed men roaming the island, in cars and pickup trucks, looking for animals to kill.

But the goat did not seem to have been shot. Maybe a broken leg. It unsettled me.

When I got to the car I leaned up against the hatchback a moment. From the small cooler in the back of the car I retrieved a lemon Fanta, still cold, and sucked it down. Then I drove back to the village, left my car in the lot, and began the walk back to my father's. I bought two cheese pies at the bakery at the village's entrance, and this is where I ran into a distressed Mira. She was sitting on a bench, drinking a juice. Her hair was damp and combed straight, close to her head. She wore cut-off shorts and a tank top. She was not flirtatious. She didn't bother with pleasantries but asked if I'd seen Nefeli. I hadn't. She'd just checked my father's house and Aris's father's too. "I need to find her. Will you take me?" She held up a small bakery bag, saying she'd bought Nefeli her favorite cookies. She looked dazed as she offered me one, and for more than a brief moment I convinced myself I had imagined the previous night. Or worse: that it had been a mistake.

At my car, Mira crawled into the passenger seat as if crawling into a bed. After a while, she sat up straight and braided her damp hair, which was already beginning to dry in waves. I tried to make conversation, if only to ease the tension I felt coming from her, but she was distracted, staring out the window. We drove the rest of that winding road in silence.

19

Mira

When we neared the cabin, which I never would have found on my own, up several unmarked winding roads, the Captain parked next to a large shrub and we walked the rest of the way quietly, side by side. Even had I known how to find it, the Fiat would never have made it. Then I followed him up the steps leading to the cottage, which was smaller than I remembered, an old, stone shepherd's dwelling, endless terraced hills in the background, a large patio off the side. She'd painted the doors and wooden shutters bright blue, and on the three white steps leading to the house were those stenciled blue scorpions. "Hello?" we said. The Captain pushed open the door, and I felt powerful sense of déjà vu.

But she was not there. The clouds had cleared and the bright haze hurt my eyes, which met the Captain's briefly. The dreamlike night had offered a thin barrier, one that didn't exist in sunlight, and it seemed inconceivable that only hours ago I had wrapped my legs around his body. I looked away, and we walked in, taking in the space.

Bees swarmed everywhere, in and out of the open window of the cottage, around the door, in her kitchen where she'd left a sticky jar of honey on the table. I covered my hand with the striped dish towel that hung on the wall and placed it outside, away from the house. On the patio there was an easel but nothing on it. Behind the cottage was a small herb garden, plots of flowers. I mentioned my surprise that Nefeli was interested in gardening, and the Captain told me his father often tended to them.

Back inside, I surveyed the place. The stone walls were painted white, and built into them were little cove-like shelves, which housed a small camp stove, a duffel bag, a few notebooks. There were two green wooden chairs covered with embroidered pillows, several bottles of water, a cold cup of coffee, an oily film on the top. In another little cove were two double beds, flowered sheets. I flopped down on one and looked out the window at a spectacular view of the terraced hills, the sea visible in the far distance. I didn't realize she had this view.

The Captain watched me carefully. "You okay?" he asked. I shrugged and told him yes. He studied my face a moment. "I swear," I added. Then said he was going to walk down to his father's hives, and he disappeared around the back of the cottage. I felt a twist in my chest.

"Maybe she's gone back to Athens," he said, but I think we both knew she hadn't. All this time, I had thought Nefeli had been performing *health* for me, but I knew now that she had been performing death. And her anger with me stemmed from my inability to tell the difference; my inability, or my refusal, to see the gesture for what it truly was.

They say when you've experienced intolerable pain, an intense injury, your body becomes oversensitized. Even taking a shower can feel painful on your skin. I imagine it's the same with emotional pain, with rejection, with grief, both the way it can re-emerge and the things we do to shield ourselves from it. I placed the small bag of cookies on the little table, sat down on the bed, my head in my hands.

Soon, from outside the cottage, I heard the Captain calling to me, but when I tried to answer, my voice cracked. No sound would emerge. I heard him come inside.

"Mira?"

"Yeah," I said, finally. I was still on the bed, head propped in my hands, looking out the window.

"One of the hives has been knocked over," he said.

"I think we should go," I said.

The drive back to the village I barely registered, so immersed was I in replaying moments from the night before, from hours before, from Nefeli's cottage and the world framed from her bedroom window, all blazing white like the marble quarry, like the bright, low moon. When we returned to the village, the Captain looked first to the sky, which had cleared, though the dark clouds still hung over the other end of the island, near the port. Then he looked back to me. I walked to my car, across the lot, thanking him for his help. He urged me to stay the night. "Please don't drive back to the port. Rest awhile."

"It doesn't matter," I said. "She's gone."

We did not hug or kiss goodbye, but he placed one hand on my shoulder and the other along my waist and told me to be careful, to get some rest. I was confused but also relieved to not have to talk about what had happened between us, to just have let it happen, to let it be. Things did not feel much different, as if we'd always had this world between us, a large, airy house overlooking the sea, a space we had entered through different doors to find each other sitting underneath a large bay window reading the paper, or at the kitchen table, drinking coffee, our bodies drawing naturally together. I was not sure how I felt about it myself. Somehow it seemed inevitable. Yet perhaps my feelings were colored by my worry about Nefeli, because I felt the sense of an ending, though an ending of what I wasn't sure.

I was distraught by impermanence, by lack of solidity. *I am fugitive, I am nothing.* I couldn't get it out of my head, as if someone else were telling it to me. You are nothing. Whose are you? You belong to no one. I drove back to the port quickly, the old Fiat shaking from the speed, held together only by salt.

It never rained after all, the dark clouds raging across the sky but emptying elsewhere. It would not rain again for a long time.

*

I went back to Athens again. I boarded the ferry and after the ship had pulled away I stood on the top deck until I could no longer see the island, not even a trace. Despite my mood, the sea was soothing in its vastness, the idea that water was connecting me to places around the world: ships and beaches and shores. The history of this island was a history of glaciers and the history of glaciers is a history of life.

I was not nothing.

At the ship's concession stand I bought a beer and some potato chips. I sat back on the top deck, in the setting sun. I remember the fading light. Nearby, a man in wire-rimmed glasses and a thick sweater sat reading a contemporary Greek writer, a book about two lovers in an email exchange. He caught me looking at him and smiled, inviting me to sit, but I declined. I thought of course of the Captain, those long routes in the Pacific, when he was younger, that he had told me about. His resistance to staying in one place.

While my parents were alive I felt a subconscious but powerful force that would not allow me to relocate to Greece, that somehow moving to the land they had left to give themselves, and me, what they saw as a better life, would be a betrayal. I could see my mother standing on the roof, her hands on her hips, *We sacrifice so much so you can end up back here?* Each time I returned I left pieces of my history around the city. A suitcase of things at Aris's. What I've left in taxi cabs alone could fill the shelves of my apartment: a bottle of wine and a mobile phone and several books and bags of gifts; books everywhere, really—on the metro, in a café, in a rented flat; scarves in tavernas and T-shirts and bathing suits in island hotel rooms. A bag of clothes in a rented apartment, a bottle of shampoo, a stack of postcards. A journal, almost filled, the worst and most embarrassing loss of all.

Yet I think they knew my work and my heart would take me back here for good. My father was already retired and my mother nearly so. They had saved the way only a certain generation of immigrants can save, they had stashed cash not only in banks and in this apartment, but all over the house. After their deaths I had found it everywhere. And that spacious brick home in Chicago was worth an exorbitant amount, more than they had ever dreamed, but I had been reluctant to sell it. Now it seemed to belong to another world.

*

Back in Athens, I looked carefully at Nefeli's paintings, the ones I hadn't yet displayed. One depicted the back of a woman, long black hair, sitting in a chair looking out a small window onto a hilly landscape. On the floor is something blue. I stared at it until I thought it might move, and then I walked away from the painting, feeling shaken up. I left them propped up around the room, as if they were fresh.

After my class, Rami waited for me outside the squat, wanting to talk about his graphic novel. So far, it was only images. "I don't know which language to use to tell the story," he said. "The one that's hardest, or easiest?" I'm not sure if he meant skill or pain. I told him he should write in the language in which he feels most at home. "Your book could always be translated," I said, and his face opened up then, as though I'd told him some giant secret. This must be part of the pleasure of having children, of watching the world reveal itself to them in simple and magnificent ways. For a kid like Rami, whose situational possibilities were currently limited, in limbo, the opening of the artistic and intellectual was no small thing. For any of us, really.

Rami's fourteenth birthday was in a week. I reminded him I knew, and his brow furrowed. He looked at his feet before looking up at me, a wan smile.

"We'll have to all do something special," I said.

"Yeah," he said. Then he did something out of character. He

flung himself to me, not his usual, boyish one-armed hug, but wrapping his arms around me. I hugged him back.

Maybe I shouldn't have mentioned it, this marker of time. It's nearly impossible for the mind to reshape what was supposed to be a temporary situation into a permanent one. I worry now that my mentioning this somehow changed the course of events, or that my talk of multiple homes put ideas in his head, or that something I had said, somehow, caused what happened next.

*

A few days later, Dimitra called, nearly hysterical. *Mira, Mira, Mira mou,* she said, in tears, and I knew that Rami was gone.

"He got tired of waiting," Dimitra said. And then she repeated it, more to herself. Perhaps there was some truth to this, that Rami, knowing he would eventually leave, simply wanted to get it over with. But I think that Rami, caught between his life here and a new life in Germany with his brother and aunt, could not bear an official goodbye. Still, I couldn't believe he was gone.

I went to Dimitra and Fady. They were angry at Leila, who had known, but she herself was so upset, inconsolable, sobbing like a toddler, they couldn't be too angry. And Fady. Fady was bereft. "I knew it would happen, I knew it wasn't forever," he kept saying. But even more, they—we—were worried. Who had he gone with, and how? Where was he? Was he safe? It was maddening. Dimitra sent me messages in the middle of the night, worried.

Three days later, the same day Rami called Dimitra to tell her he'd safely made it—how, exactly, we still do not know—the novelist phoned to tell me two German hikers had found Nefeli's jeans and T-shirt and the scarf she'd been wearing in her hair, all folded neatly atop a stone, near the edge of a cliff, a short hike from her small cottage. On a large rock she had stenciled a blue scorpion. It had not rained for weeks, the wind had been still, and one of those scorpion-women had been scorched into the ground. Nearby the ground smoldered, but the hikers put it out before it became a fire.

But she herself had vanished. As if she had alighted into air: from body to vapor, from earth to sky.

I asked the novelist what the church would do if it were a suicide. Easy, he said. It's not a suicide. And the body? I asked. Don't worry, he said.

I dreamt of scorpions again, skittering across the floor, scurrying over my torso, my back. I woke sweating, my heart racing, and went outside to look at the moon, cold as marble. But I was relieved to be alone. I glanced at my phone. A new message from Rami: a photo of the sketchbook I'd given him before he'd ever shown me his drawings. Then another: a silly little stuffed panda I'd also given him: first perched on a skateboard, then sitting in a café chair, then another looking out a windowsill at the rain. *Watch the mail,* it said.

A few days later in the building lobby I found a large box addressed to me, from Germany. A manuscript, a bound photocopy of Rami's book. The rest was in Arabic and a little bit of English. It remained untitled. There was a Post-it on the front that said, *Dear M, Thank you and I hope Fady will read it to you!! Maybe you can help me with a title!*

My heart was pounding. I'd seen sections of it, drawings, a

series of frames: kids eating ice cream, kicking a ball around, sitting in desks in school. What I found so impressive was the way he read and rendered faces, the subtle way the slant of an eyebrow could show surprise or fear or anger or laughter, the way a flick of a smile could be full of subtext. But I had not seen him finish a story, give something a beginning, middle, and end.

The story was about a group of friends, a boy named Rami at their center, whose homes were, day by day, disappearing. First went their school. They arrived one day to the gymnasium and it was gone. But Rami never resorts to realism: the school was not destroyed by bombs or shells or even natural disaster. Each day more disappeared until he pictured only an empty landscape, as if the structure never existed at all. No trace of books or pens of chalkboards, no computers or broken windows. Just cleanly excised from the landscape; only bitter orange and loquat trees remained.

And then the language disappears. Images: kids roaming the city, watching movies, painting a mural on the movie house—the girl with the thick black glasses signs her name in Greek—and then the movie house disappears too. Video games whose landscapes look just like their own. Then houses begin to disappear, some of the children opening apartment doors to find only air, nothing behind the gates, beyond their gardens, maybe only a stray toy strewn on the ground until the buildings are gone. When Rami realizes he is alone with the city, along with the girl with the black glasses, neither of them returns home. They don't want to see. We see the pair walking away from the city, to a place we do not know. A small toy panda peeks out from the girl's backpack.

I sat with the book for hours, reading it front to back, back to front, paging through, often settling for fifteen minutes on just one image. By instinct, I pulled out my phone to text Nefeli, and was hit again by the ache of loss.

When Nefeli disappeared, instead of the documentary footage juxtaposed with scenes from the outdoors, the screen displayed only words—photographed images of pages from her journals dating back to 1970; photos of the graffiti outside her studio; fragments of laments, more texts from poems. Other days only a few words from Cavafy's unfinished poem "Hidden." As if she'd planned it all.

*

My mother stood next to me at Nefeli's funeral. My father next to her, very still, looking straight ahead, but a relaxed expression on his face, as if he were watching a good movie or reading. He glanced at me, his eyes so deep and calm. I turned behind me to look at the faces, past and present; so many people in various states of shock and grief.

My mother kept turning to face me, nearly mischievous, as if she wanted to talk. She had candies in her purse and she was fussing with them, unwrapping them. She touched my cheek, she wiped my tears. Her eyelashes, with mascara, were curled; her thick hair cut to her shoulders with only a hint of gray. Her young self, in a sense, but in her good black dress, her current haircut.

My father, to her right, was exactly the self I'd remembered before he'd died; he even wore the new maroon sweater I'd bought him for his birthday. Dimitra and Leila and Fady lined up too. Leila's eyebrows were brown again but she'd dyed a blue streak in her hair. Dimitra, behind me, kept her hand on my shoulder.

We owe the dead a lot.

What we knew: Each day Nefeli went up the hill behind her cottage, past the bee hives, past the old church, past the point where the earth was scorched and black, and worked on her installation, a companion piece to the one in Athens—another larger, cruder looking megaphone she built from wood, from two-by-fours. She had met a few young men at the port looking for work. They helped carve the wood, treat it, I imagine. She had always made friends instantly.

I went back to the island, and it took me most of the morning to find it in those hills.

Larger than the megaphones of the exhibit, this one pointed straight upward. For a moment I wondered whether she had installed a camera inside, to project the passing clouds on those screens at the museum. But this wasn't the point, I knew. Nefeli wanted this out here, removed, silently pointing up to the limitless sky.

There was no note. This was what remained.

I sat on the ground, amid tiny little purple flowers, scrubby grass, sun-baked earth. There was a little breeze, and I swear I could hear the eerie harmonies I'd heard down by the sails. I listened closely, to see if I could distinguish the sounds playing in my mind or those outside it, but it did not matter. I sprawled out beneath her structure and lay still for an hour, nearly feeling her hand in the small of my back again. By the time I stood to leave, my eyes were red and my face was puffy, and I don't know if I felt better or simply different.

Eventually others would visit it as well.

Later we'd hear from the local builder—a young guy who played music in the clubs at night, his voice like butter—that he'd delivered the supplies for her with a dump truck, shared his tools, helped her and Nikos build. Some days he brought them sandwiches. Often he came back for her, to pick her up, to take her there, when Nikos did not. As plain as day. I talked to him and his father, the owner of the business, one late afternoon at Thanassis's. They found her together, her body, that is, as they were driving around in the truck with Nikos. No wonder Nikos was so distressed.

My god. I missed her.

One night back in Athens I had dinner with Fady and Dimitra, and Leila came out of her bedroom holding her phone, showed us Rami's earnest face. He'd dyed his hair blue, too. We waved and talked excitedly, and when she went back into her bedroom to continue the conversation the three of us cried.

Later, Leila described his new apartment, his new city, that he said he was still waiting for the sun to come out but otherwise he liked it. After spending so many years in such bright light, the grayness was hard to get used to. He got along with his cousins, his aunt, his brother, but Leila said he wanted to talk about Athens. Leila saw I'd been crying and she gave me a hug, her own eyes wet with tears. "He misses you," she said. "You know what he told me? That you look like his mother."

Then, that evening, Aris called me.

The novelist had been planning a big party on the island for his seventy-fifth birthday. I assumed this was why Aris was calling. I had planned to go but had not considered the complications. The novelist himself had said he wasn't really in the mood.

"Mira?" Aris's voice quivered. I knew him so well on the phone: after all those years, it had become our greatest intimacy.

"Hi, Aris," I said. I kept my voice low, gentle. Something was wrong. There was silence, and he then began to sob. How can I explain to you how I felt at that moment? I did not feel rancor or spite or jealousy. Whatever I felt of that was long gone. I felt a great warmth, to be honest. I may have been angry at Aris, and hurt by the breakup that felt so sudden, but I realized I had already forgiven him, forgave him the way you'd forgive a parent who frequently disappoints you. Despite the pain, it was the right thing between us, to part ways. I think that accounts for so many problems between people. The insistence that there should be no pain. For me he became mentor, parent, lover, friend. But even with all that, or maybe because of all that, little room remained for that mysterious, continuous thing.

The knot in my throat blocked me from speaking. The truth of life is always stranger than the truth of fiction, and all this I'm telling you is true. I listened to Aris sob into the phone. It seemed the right thing to do. It seemed the right thing, period, talking to him right after he had held his daughter for the first time. *This* was love, too: so open and generous and alive. There are so many ways to love. How is it we only have one word for it? I might not have been his great love, if there was such a thing. That was okay. The demand for reciprocity was bizarre, insane. And impossible.

"Eva's okay?" I asked. It was the first time I had said her name.

"Exhausted, but okay," he said. "C-section."

"You're at the hospital now?" I asked.

"She's so tiny."

"How wonderful," I said, and I truly meant it. As if all those years together were still leading up to this moment.

"Mi mou," he said. He hadn't used this nickname in months, years. So much in those words. I am frightened I am sorry I am overjoyed I am alive.

"It's okay, Ari mou," I said. "*Se filo.*"

20

The Captain

After Nefeli's funeral the day was bright. I saw Mira up ahead, a small figure in black. Her hair was a bit lighter now, perhaps from the sun, worn in an elaborate braid wrapped around her head, the way Ifigenia sometimes wore hers to soccer practice. Behind her, I saw the journalist-singer and her husband, their daughter. I wondered what had happened to the boy whom I know Mira loved.

"Hi, you," I said. I leaned in to greet her with a kiss on each cheek. When I touched her waist I felt something flutter inside me.

"Hi," she said, as she pulled away. Her lip trembled. She did not say, *It's been a long time*, and I was grateful. Her usual self, her serious face, as if I greeted her at funerals every day.

There were hundreds there, it seemed. I caught a glimpse of Aris with his father across the crowd. My father refused to come: I don't think he could accept it. He wanted to keep her there, with him, up in the house, her megaphone up on the hill. When

I spoke to him the night before, though he seemed bewildered, I understood that he had loved Nefeli, and even though she did not love him in the same way, she loved him too. Losing her was more painful than I had previously understood. They were both difficult people, which made people fall in love with them left and right.

I did not want to say *It's good to see you.* I wanted to say *May her memory be eternal,* but I did not. "Let's go somewhere," I said instead. "Let's have a beer."

Her eyes were red. She glanced back at her friends. "Later today?" she said.

We agreed to meet not right at the port but at an old café a bit farther away, on the water next to a small beach, where my father's friend Minas kept his old fishing boat.

I arrived first and sat in the shade. I was alone in the café, and on the beach next to it a young woman and her dog played with a stick. When Mira arrived she didn't say anything but instead sat right down and smiled. It felt odd to be sitting across from her like that, facing her. The waiter smiled at Mira as if they shared a secret. We ordered beers, the waiter brought pistachios. We spoke.

When it began to rain, something strange happened. We both instinctively moved our chairs to the long end of the table, which was covered under the awning. As if choreographed. The sea facing us. At that moment she turned sideways, and smiled. Conspiratorial. Then she turned her head back to the water. Together we stared out into that openness, continuing our conversation, side by side, as if nothing had happened, but of course everything had.